Praise for the Series

"This heartwarming, swooning and for true love."
~InD'Tale

"This pleasant tale will reward readers with the dance of life for a resounding happily-ever-after."
~InD'Tale Magazine review of *Not Your Match*

"The witty dialogue and the emotion that slowly enraptures the reader makes this book a gem."
~InD'Tale Magazine review of *Mix 'N Match*

"Expect solid writing, likeable characters, plausible fun plots, slick descriptions and wonderful romance."
~Lisa Swinton, award-winning author

"Devoured it in an evening!"
~Laura D. Bastian, author of *Echoes of Summer*

"Talk about book hangovers!"
~Jaclyn Weist, author of *Ring of Truth*

"Heart-melting romance."
~Liz Stone, reader

"Lindzee Armstrong knocks it out of the park again! Fun and entertaining, yet clean."
~Bre, reader

A NO MATCH FOR LOVE NOVELLA

OTHER BOOKS BY LINDZEE ARMSTRONG

No Match for Love Series
Strike a Match
Meet Your Match
Miss Match
Mix 'N Match
Mistletoe Match

Sunset Plains Romance Series
Cupcakes and Cowboys
Twisters and Textbooks

Other Works
Chasing Someday
First Love, Second Choice

A No Match for Love Novella

#1 BEST-SELLING AUTHOR
LINDZEE ARMSTRONG

Snowflake Press

Copyright © 2016 by Lindzee Armstrong
Published by Snowflake Press

All rights reserved. This book is a work of fiction. Names, characters, places, and incidents are either a product of the author's imagination or are used fictitiously. Any resemblance to actual events, locales, or persons, living or dead, is entirely coincidental. No part of this book can be reproduced in any form or by electronic or mechanical means, including information storage and retrieval systems, without the express written permission of the author.

Cover Design by Novak Illustrations
Interior Design by Snowflake Press
Edited by Kelley Gerschke

Tooele, UT
ISBN 978-0-9981667-0-4
Library of Congress Control Number 2016920265

*To my amazing Sweet 'N Spicy Readers,
who provide me invaluable support
on this crazy writing journey.
I couldn't do it without you amazing people!*

Chapter One

Kate dropped onto the couch in the nurse's break room, her legs collapsing beneath her as she struggled to keep her eyes open. Sixteen hours since she'd been outside the hospital. It felt like sixteen days.

She'd stay for sixteen more if it meant not having to play a nurse-slash-doormat to Beau. But she'd worked her three days of twelve-hour shifts, and she'd have to spend the next four days at home.

She sniffed her scrub top, then winced at the sour smell. She'd slipped in a puddle of vomit when rushing to a Code Blue, and even though she'd changed her top, the scent clung to her. And maybe a bit of amniotic fluid, too. She'd had to catch a baby when a crowning mom couldn't wait for the doctor.

"That bad, huh?"

Kate glanced up at Liza, who's frizzy gray-streaked hair and rumpled blue scrubs suggested she was as tired as Kate felt.

Strike a Match

"I can't believe three nurses called in sick," Kate said. "That's got to be some sort of record for one shift."

"There's not enough hand sanitizer in the world to keep the stomach flu away forever." Liza spun the dial on her locker door. "I can't wait to go home and take a long, hot bath. I've been here fourteen hours. What about you?"

"Sixteen." And she'd spent the last two comforting a mom who'd lost a baby—full term, with no complications other than a missing fetal heartbeat. Kate had held back tears as she helped the grief-stricken parents bathe and dress their baby, then place a pink bow on her head. Kate had spent ten minutes crying in the bathroom before collecting herself enough to finish her final rounds.

Liza winced in sympathy. "At least you have that handsome husband of yours waiting for you at home. Mine is grabbing takeout tonight. I told him I was too tired to cook."

It took everything in Kate not to laugh at the idea of Beau grabbing takeout. He was a lot of things, but a doting husband definitely wasn't one of them.

He's in pain, Kate reminded herself for the millionth time. Beau broke his back in a roofing accident only two months into their marriage. Nothing had been the same since then.

"It must be nice to have a husband at home who can hold down the fort while you're working," Liza continued. "One year until Keith can retire and do the same. I'm counting down the minutes."

Kate would just be grateful if Beau hadn't created more work for her. When she'd left that morning at four o'clock—Beau still snoring loudly in their bed—the dishes had overflowed in the sink, the counters hadn't been wiped down in two days, and three baskets of unfolded laundry sat at the foot of their bed. In the past, she would've suggested he help pick up around the place. But the days of silent treatment—or worse, the verbal cut-downs she'd receive for the suggestion—had stopped being worth it long ago.

You love him, she reminded herself. But after six years, she was so exhausted.

"See you Monday?" Liza asked. "I think we're working the same shift."

"Yeah. It's your last week, right?"

"Yes, and it can't come soon enough. I'm getting too old for these insanely long days. Are you sure you don't want to come with me? They're still hiring."

The offer was beyond tempting. Liza had been hired by a pediatrician's office, where she'd work five eight-hour days and only one weekend a month. It would be so nice to have an excuse to be gone each day, to have energy to pick up around the house when she got home. But it also wouldn't have the overtime pay of the hospital. "Thanks, but I need to stay here."

"Well, the offer stands. No promises, but I'd put in a good word for you. See you Monday." Liza gave a little wave and left the break room.

Kate pulled her backpack out of a locker. The glowing screen of her phone showed Beau had texted her twenty-three times in the last sixteen hours. She wondered what she'd done wrong this time, and how much money Beau had spent in retribution. His disability checks barely covered their utilities and didn't come close to covering what he spent each month on beer and cigarettes. But he still complained whenever she picked up extra shifts to help with the financial strain.

He'd be mad when she walked in the front door without calling him first. But the last half hour of peace and quiet was worth it. She clung to the hope that the man she married was still somewhere inside the Beau hardened by years of chronic pain.

Kate sank onto the bus stop bench outside the hospital, a few mosquitoes buzzing around the glowing streetlight. The California heat had finally died down with the onset of fall, and a light breeze cooled the sticky perspiration on her skin. She ran a weary hand over her hair, smoothing the dark brown strands back into her ponytail. Her auburn roots were starting to show again. She'd have to get up before Beau in the morning and dye the red away.

The bus was on time for a change. Kate gratefully took a seat near the front and leaned her head against the window. Maybe she'd sleep in the spare room tonight. Beau snored so loudly, and his constant tossing and turning kept her awake. If she sneaked out after he fell asleep, he'd never know.

"Isn't this your stop, honey?"

Kate jerked awake, forcing her eyelids open despite the way they burned. "Yes, thank you."

"You look exhausted. Go home and get some rest, okay? They work you too hard at that hospital."

"I'll do my best. Goodnight." Kate stumbled on the last step but caught herself before falling.

The three blocks home might as well be a marathon. Every painful step rubbed the blister on her foot raw. The sun had set hours ago, the dim streetlights illuminating the cracked and buckling sidewalk. Kate let her head droop as she struggled to keep her eyes open. The route was so familiar she could probably walk it in her sleep. Not that she was eager to try.

She turned the corner and squinted at the sudden change in light intensity. Her eyes protested at the flashing blue-and-red, the sandpaper feeling making them water. She fought against the pain for three seconds, blinking rapidly, before her vision finally cleared.

Two blocks down, in the middle of the cul-de-sac where she lived, were four police cars and two fire trucks. The next door neighbor's teenage son had probably been caught vandalizing the high school again.

And then she saw the smoke.

Her heart stopped beating, then raced in her chest as she struggled to breathe. Black smoke poured from the windows of her small rambler. Flames licked at the wood siding, swallowing it up like a hungry lion.

Kate's feet pounded against the pavement as she ran past the neighbors standing on their front steps, past Old Mr. Hillman's yippy Pomeranian, and toward the house that held everything she owned. Her grandfather had built that house. She'd been raised there. The hope chest he'd given her for high school graduation would never survive that blaze. All her furniture, clothing, and mementos were being eaten alive by the inferno.

And then she thought of one more thing that might be inside that house. Beau.

No! She pushed herself to run faster. Guilt slammed against her for every negative thought she'd had about him today.

Her hands grasped at the bulky yellow-and-black fire coat of the first fireman she reached. Soot covered his face but couldn't hide the cleft in his chin. He was perhaps in his late twenties, with startling blue eyes that pierced through the dark.

"My husband," Kate gasped. Her sides ached from her two-block sprint and she was pretty sure her blister was bleeding. "Was he inside?"

She'd wanted out for years, ever since it became clear the accident had stolen her husband. But not like this. Never like this. Her knees buckled and the fireman grabbed her arm, his grip firm and steady. She clung to him, the world spinning.

Beau had to have been inside when the fire started. He never went anywhere. She tried to picture him hobbling out of the house with his cane but couldn't.

"Are you the owner of this house?" The fireman's voice was deep, but still somehow soft.

Kate nodded, her breath coming in gasps. "Yes. Kaitlynn Monroe. My husband has back problems and walks with a cane. He's usually watching TV in the living room or sleeping in the bedroom."

The fireman covered her hand where it grasped his coat. She did the same thing when trying to comfort grieving parents.

She should've been here to help him. Should've insisted she couldn't stay on shift for an extra four hours. Planets collided in her mind and the rubble would bury her alive.

"Is he okay?" Kate asked, her voice a squeak.

"I'm so sorry, Mrs. Monroe." The silver nameplate across his left breast pocket flashed in the moonlight, and she could just make out the word *Coleman*. "We got him out of the house, but it was already too late. The paramedics couldn't revive him."

Kate stumbled. This time Fireman Coleman wasn't quick enough and she fell to her knees, the blacktop cutting through the thin fabric of her scrubs and sending sharp pains up her legs.

Beau was dead. It was over.

Fireman Coleman crouched next to her and whispered soothing words. She might've been on the ground for five seconds or five hours when a police officer walked over. Together, he and Fireman Coleman led her to the back of an ambulance. Kate obediently sat down and someone wrapped a blanket around her shoulders. A steaming cup of something hot was pressed into her hands.

Dead. Gone. Just like that baby she'd helped deliver five hours ago.

"Is there anyone I can call for you?" Fireman Coleman asked.

Kate looked up, surprised to see him standing just outside the ambulance. Had he been there this entire time? The police officer and paramedic stood nearby as well.

"No," Kate choked. "There's no one." Liza was her only real friend, and she didn't even know her phone number. Beau had been Kate's entire life—for better or worse—for six years.

She should've been here. She could've helped him out of the house, or maybe prevented the fire in the first place. He must've fallen asleep with a cigarette in his hand, like she'd warned him against so many times.

The tears fell down her cheeks, hot and heavy. Fireman Coleman rested his hands on his hips, his blue eyes heavy with sympathy. Kate's shoulders shook as shivering overtook her body. Beau couldn't be dead. She should ask to see the body, just to make sure. Was he still here, in the back of the other ambulance, or had they taken him to the medical examiner's office? Surely they'd be required to perform an autopsy.

"She's in shock," the paramedic murmured. Another blanket fell around her shoulders.

So this was what shock felt like. She'd be more sympathetic when her next patient experienced it. The frantic shivers jarred Kate's sore muscles. She closed her eyes tightly, struggling to control the muscle spasms.

"There's no one who can be with you right now?" Fireman Coleman pressed. "A family member, perhaps? Or a friend?"

"I'm . . . I'm not sure." Kate wiped at her cheeks. Her father was in prison, her mother probably dead.

She didn't have any friends outside of the hospital. Beau had isolated her from everyone.

"I'm so sorry," Fireman Coleman repeated. "I'm so, so sorry."

It's over, Kate thought. Beau was gone. Forever. The tears fell, thicker and harder.

Fireman Colman crouched beside her again, murmuring "I'm sorry" like he didn't know what else to do. His blue eyes glistened in the moonlight, his lips turned down in a sympathetic frown. She wondered what he would say if he knew what the tears were really for. If he understood what emotion tumbled through her body until she shook with the intensity of it.

Relief.

Chapter Two

EIGHTEEN MONTHS LATER

Kate flipped the flag outside an exam room to green, then headed to the nurse's station in the center of the pediatrician's office. She flopped into a chair and woke up her tablet, double checking that her notes had synced for the doctor.

"Behind on your charting again?" Liza teased.

"Always," Kate said. But she enjoyed the pace of the pediatrician's office much more than that of the hospital. She'd forever be grateful to Liza for getting her this job.

"The afternoon should be slow," Liza said. "We aren't overbooked for once. Might even get out of here on time for once."

Kate nodded. A year and a half ago, an early day would've filled her with dread. But now it meant relaxing on the couch with Chinese takeout and Netflix while ignoring the guilt that nudged her for not missing Beau.

She still wasn't used to the creaks and groans of her new home. It had taken nearly six months for the insurance companies—both homeowners and life—to verify the police report that confirmed the fire had accidentally started when Beau fell asleep with a lit cigarette in his hand and blood alcohol levels off the charts. Then it had taken another ten months for the old house to be knocked down and a new one built in its place. She'd thought about selling the property and moving elsewhere, but that would've meant taking out a loan she couldn't afford. She still missed the old house and the good memories from her childhood. But the bad ones from her marriage to Beau had weighed on her every day, a dark aura around the place that she hadn't known how to shake.

Some days she barely thought of Beau. Other times she hated herself for being so much happier with him gone. The last year and a half had felt like sunlight after a long winter, but loneliness had begun to creep in as well. It had taken a lot of courage to admit she wanted another relationship—this time, a healthy one. Without Beau around to cloud her thinking, she'd realize that the warning signs had been there even before his accident. She'd just ignored them.

"So, have you met with that dating agency yet?" Liza asked, almost as though she could read Kate's thoughts.

Kate tapped her fingernail on the keyboard. "My appointment is later today." The nerves clawed at her insides, along with the fear that threatened to choke her. Dating meant possibly ending up with another Beau. And given the choice, she'd rather be lonely.

"What's wrong? I thought you were really excited about it."

"I am. But I'm nervous, too." Kate had felt the pull toward another relationship for a few months now, but she couldn't trust her own judgment when it came to men. Not after her disastrous marriage.

When she'd heard about Toujour, a professional matchmaking agency, it had seemed like the perfect solution. All of Toujour's clients were carefully vetted. Extensive personal profiles and background checks ensured only those serious about a relationship—and ready for one—became a client. They boasted a high success rate that left her hopeful. One of the receptionists at the clinic had even met her fiancé through the agency.

But now Kate just felt nervous. Guilty. How could she even consider moving on after a mere eighteen months? She'd thought she'd put Beau behind her, but thinking about dating had brought up a lot of her old issues.

"Oh, Kate." Liza wrapped an arm around her shoulders and squeezed. "I'm sure you miss your husband very much. But he'd want you to move on and be happy."

Kate knew for a fact that Beau would want—no, expect—the exact opposite. But it had been easier to play the part of a grieving widow than to explain to everyone just how emotionally abusive and manipulative Beau had become.

"Go," Liza said. "You deserve to be happy."

Kate blinked back tears. "Okay."

For the next few hours, Kate administered vaccines to kids, handed out suckers, and calmed nervous parents. But in the back of her mind, she kept thinking about her upcoming appointment with Toujour. Her matchmaker, Brooke, had emailed Kate the initial profile and questionnaire last week. Maybe Brooke would already have a match picked out. Kate's heart quickened, and she could almost hear Beau yelling at her for not missing him more.

This isn't about Beau, she reminded herself. *This is about me.*

As Kate worked on entering the last patient notes into the computer, the overhead lights flickered off, leaving only the emergency lights on. The clinic was officially closed.

Liza flopped into the chair next to Kate. "You're going, right?"

Kate's heart might pound out of her chest, but she nodded. "Yeah. I'm going."

"Good." Liza flipped the top on a can of soda and took a chug. "Make sure they set you up with a nice man. Someone who will be sensitive to your unique circumstances."

If anyone was insensitive, it was Kate. What kind of wife was glad her husband was gone? Maybe she didn't know how to have a healthy relationship. Maybe she was incapable of being attracted to someone who wasn't all wrong for her. But she owed it to herself to at least try.

"I'm sure they know what they're doing," Kate said. She saved her last note and shut down the computer. "I'm off."

Liza eyed Kate's red and white scrubs with the black Mickey Mouse ears. "You aren't changing?"

Kate tugged at her top. "There isn't time, and I'm just meeting with the matchmaker. Is it weird that I'm not dressing up for this?" She ran a hand through her auburn hair, pulled back in its customary ponytail. She'd dyed it back to her natural color the week after Beau died. "I don't know what I'm doing."

"You look great," Liza said quickly. She grasped Kate's hand and squeezed. "And I'll take you shopping before your first date."

Kate nodded. She'd lived in scrubs for so long, she wasn't even sure what else was in her closet. The only nice dress she owned was the black one she'd worn to Beau's funeral. "See you tomorrow."

Strike a Match

"Good luck." Liza gave a little wave.

Kate swallowed back the nerves and climbed into the used car she'd bought mere days after Beau's passing. Without the weekly cases of beer and cartons of cigarettes, making the payments hadn't been too difficult. She pulled into a nearly empty parking lot, her heart beating in her throat until she wanted to throw up.

A bell tinkled when she opened the front door, making her jump. The lobby was small, with half a dozen empty chairs lined up underneath the picture window. A strong spicy-sweet scent nearly overpowered her nose. Instrumental music played quietly through speakers, and a sleek black reception desk sat empty at the front. A board filled with wedding announcements for happy, smiling couples lined one wall—a pretty good advertisement, Kate had to concede. She quickly picked her coworkers invitation out of the collage.

Kate walked toward the desk, hands clasped together to hide the trembling. At least no one sat in the lobby to scoff at her scrubs. She must be the last appointment of the day.

She shifted from foot to foot, then checked her watch. The room was uncomfortably quiet except for the music. She peered down a short hallway that obviously led to somewhere, but didn't see anyone. The desk didn't have a bell to ring.

It was a sign. She should run right out that door and never come back. Kate took a tentative step away from the desk, glancing at the door, then stopped.

No. She'd already paid the first month's subscription, and leaving would mean letting Beau win. It would mean admitting he'd broken her.

A woman walked into the room, several manila files stacked precariously in her arms. She let out a gasp, her eyes widening as she stared at Kate. The scrubs had definitely been a mistake. Next time, she'd dig in the bottom of her closet for a pair of jeans and T-shirt at the very least.

"Hi," Kate said.

The woman lurched forward. The unexpected movement upset the delicate balance, and files tumbled to the floor, their contents spilling everywhere.

"Crap," the woman said, struggling to crouch down in her restrictive pencil skirt.

Kate dropped to the floor and started gathering up the files. "I'm so sorry. I didn't mean to startle you."

The woman was young, perhaps still in college, with sparkling green eyes and a friendly expression. "No, it's my fault. Things have been a little slow lately, so you surprised me, that's all. I was going to add older paper charts to the computer system." She clamped her lips shut, as though she'd said something she shouldn't have.

Strike a Match

Kate picked up the last folder and rose, handing it to the woman. She was dying to ask why business was slow—and what that meant for Kate's dating pool at Toujour—but it didn't seem polite. "I have an appointment with Brooke."

"Right. I did see that when I went over the schedule this morning. I'm Lianna." She dropped the file folders onto the desk and bent over, clicking on the computer screen. "I'm usually really organized, I promise. Yes, I see we've got you down. I should've checked the calendar, but I was only gone a moment."

"I didn't mind waiting."

"I'm sure Brooke is expecting you. She's the best matchmaker at our firm. Let me show you to a Parlour, and I'll let her know you're here."

Kate followed Lianna down the short hallway, which opened up into a room with cubicles in the center, doorways on each side, and a glass conference room at the back. Posters of happy couples with inspirational quotes hung on the walls in between doors.

Lianna stopped at the first door and held it open. "I'll send Brooke right over," she said, white teeth gleaming as she smiled.

"Thank you." The room—or Parlour, as Lianna had called it—was small, but cozy. Two black armchairs framed a coffee table, and a vinyl-lettered quote splayed across one wall. Kate clutched at her purse strap, her palms slick with moisture. She'd been in love a few times in her life, and each had ended more disastrously than the last. Her grandmother always said Kate had a nurturing spirit. All that seemed to translate into was falling into codependent relationships that left her soul bruised and battered.

That's why I'm here, she reminded herself. The professional matchmaker might just succeed where Kate had failed.

The door swung open, and Kate quickly stood. The woman before her was barely older than the receptionist, probably only in her mid-twenties. She was of average height and slender, the fitted skirt and jacket giving her a professional air. She held a laptop in the crook of one arm and extended a hand.

"Kaitlynn, I'm Brooke. It's so nice to meet you."

"You as well," Kate said, taking the hand and giving it a quick shake. Brooke sank into a chair, looking vibrant and at home. This was a woman comfortable in her own skin. Kate slowly sat down, tugging at the hem of her Mickey Mouse scrub top.

Brooke opened up the laptop, her loose brown curls bouncing with the movement. She swept her hair back over one shoulder. "I went over your profile yesterday in preparation for our meeting. Thank you for being so detailed in your answers. It helps me make the best possible matches for you."

"Of course." Kate twisted the strap of her purse, cheeks heating at the compliment. She'd felt like an idiot filling that profile out, answering all sorts of personal questions about herself and what she wanted out of life. But she'd forced herself to be honest. Nothing she'd done in the past had resulted in a successful relationship. If she wanted to find someone to share her life with—and remain happy in the process—she'd have to step outside her comfort zone.

"I'm so sorry about your husband."

Kate's hand froze on the purse strap. The questionnaire had asked about past relationships, and she'd felt it would be dishonest to leave out a prior marriage. She'd given the barest of details, not mentioning how conflicted she felt over being a widow. Kate realized she was nodding frantically. She tensed her neck muscles, forcing the movement to stop. "Thank you. It's been a year and a half now, and I'm ready to move on."

"I think you're very brave. It can't be easy to get back out there after such a traumatic loss, but I'll do everything in my power to make your journey a positive one. You're going to find love again. And I'm going to help you."

Love—Kate wasn't even sure if she knew what that word meant anymore. Had she ever truly loved Beau? She'd thought so once upon a time, but now she wasn't so sure.

"I appreciate it," Kate said. "I'm excited" —make that terrified— "to start this next chapter of my life."

"Good, because I've already found a few guys I'd like to set you up with. Three, actually. I thought we could talk about each of them, and then decide which one would be the best choice for your first date."

Brooke turned the laptop around, showing Kate the screen. Three photos were pulled up. The man on the right had a receding hairline but looked clean-cut and professional in a business suit. The man on the left wore a button-down shirt that was open at the collar, his mouth turned up in a half smile. But the photo in the middle caught her attention more than the other two combined. He wore jeans and a gray T-shirt. His skin was California tan, his face covered in just enough scruff to be sexy. Biceps strained the fabric of his shirt, and an easy smile seemed to declare *I'm a fun, happy-go-lucky guy*. He was definitely attractive—no sign of a beer gut on this guy—and if the photo was any indication, he cared about things like personal hygiene.

"Ah," Brooke said, a smile on her lips. "Which one has caught your attention?"

Kate hesitated, then pointed to the man in the middle.

"That's Taylor," Brooke said. "The two of you listed a lot of the same values on your profiles. You both ranked traits like kindness, self-reliance, and loyalty very highly. I'm actually his matchmaker, too. He's been with Toujour about two months, and I've gotten to know him pretty well. He's incredibly compassionate, which I think is something you probably need in a partner right now. But he's also strong and capable—a true gentleman in every sense of the word."

Kate's heart pounded in her chest, and she struggled to control her breathing. She squeezed her eyes shut tightly. Too soon. This was too much, too soon. She hadn't really expected to leave with a match today.

But something about those eyes . . .

"Kaitlynn?" Brooke asked gently.

Kate blinked, the name jolting her back to the present. Beau had always called her Kaitlynn. In the beginning she'd loved that he used her full name, but by the end it had grated on her nerves.

Brooke set the laptop on the coffee table and leaned forward, her arms braced on her knees, eyebrows raised in a silent question.

"Sorry," Kate said, her voice croaking on the one word. She cleared her throat. "I'm here because you're the professional, and I don't have the best track record when it comes to picking men. I trust your judgment."

"Okay." Brooke's smile brimmed with compassion. "Want me to tell you about the other two guys as well?"

"Oh. Yes, of course." She'd almost forgotten about them.

Lindzee Armstrong

Brooke pointed to the man in the suit. "James is a financial planner and very focused and driven. I thought you two might be a good match since you both value loyalty and hard work very highly. Roderick is a bit of a free spirit, but I think the two of you could balance each other out. He's adventurous, but also patient and very sensitive to others needs."

Kate tried to really look at the other two men, but her eyes kept drifting back to Taylor. The cleft in his chin reminded her of someone.

Brooke laughed. "I can tell which man intrigues you the most. I'll speak with Taylor today and see if we can arrange a date for sometime in the next week. Conflicting work schedules may present a challenge. Are you free this weekend?"

This weekend. Kate wasn't sure why, but she'd assumed this would take more time. She took a deep breath, trying to calm her breathing. She wanted this—needed this. "I'm usually off work at six on Fridays, and I'm available all Saturday."

"Great. I'll see what works for him." Brooke tapped away on the keyboard. "I thought a nice, non-threatening first date might be bowling. It'll give you lots of time to talk, but also something to focus on."

"Sounds great," Kate said. Beau had taken her bowling a few years after his accident and taunted her every gutter ball, then pouted when she actually hit the pins.

"Okay then. I'll let you know in the next day or two when and where the date will be."

Kate nodded and rose. Taylor had one of those faces—she'd probably met someone who looked like him once upon a time. She thought back to the picture and tried to imagine laughing with him in a dimly lit bowling alley as they exchanged life stories. Her stomach churned.

You want this, she reminded herself. *It'll be good for you.*

For better or worse, she was back on the market.

Chapter Three

Taylor raced up the cracked concrete steps of his childhood home, desperately hoping he wasn't too late. The afternoon beat at his back, causing sweat to bead along his hairline. Or was it from anxiety? His parents would never let him hear the end of it. Just because there were no cars lining the curb, no music or laughter emanating from the house, didn't mean he'd missed the party completely. There could be no cars because people had chosen to walk. There was no laughter because everyone was busy eating.

He tucked the present under the crook of his arm and swallowed hard, bracing himself for the disapproval he knew would soon rain down on him. But late was better than not showing up at all. Amy had needed him, whatever his parents claimed.

Taylor raised his fist and knocked. Was that the hum of the television? The sound muted, then he heard the creak of an armchair and heavy footfalls against the thick shag carpeting. Crap. He'd definitely missed the party if his dad was watching the game instead of manning the grill. The door swung open and Taylor wilted under his father's glare like he was seventeen instead of twenty-seven.

"You're late," Dad said.

"Sorry." Taylor slipped inside, shutting the door behind him. The click of the latch echoed in the quiet living room. A garbage bag leaned against the wall in the hallway, bulging with paper plates and cups.

"You missed the party," Dad said. "Your mom's near heartbroken that neither of her children were there."

"Amy wanted to come, but something came up."

Dad pierced him with a stare, then gave a knowing nod. "Uh-huh."

It had taken a straight month of begging before Amy agreed to come to the party. Taylor had driven to San Diego yesterday and picked her up since her car had been repossessed yet again. But when he got home from work that afternoon, Amy was gone. He tracked her down at a bar mere moments before a friend showed up to take her wasted self back to San Diego. But he couldn't tell his parents that. It would kill them to know Amy could've come and hadn't.

Taylor shifted from foot to foot, wishing he could just go home to his apartment and Ember, his dog. This whole day had royally sucked. "Where's Mom?"

Dad let out a grunt, sinking into his armchair. "She went outside to start a load of laundry. It's not every day your mother turns sixty, you know."

Taylor's hands tightened around the wrapped box he held. "I know."

"Her friends worked real hard planning that surprise party for her."

"I wish I could've been here."

"Are you so sure you couldn't have been?"

Taylor sighed. "Amy needed my help."

"What was it this time?"

"She wanted to come to the party, but it was too much for her." Amy had run away only days after Taylor graduated from high school and she didn't. She'd been arrested on a DUI—her first time as an adult instead of a minor—and their parents had refused to post her bail. But Taylor couldn't turn his back on his twin so easily.

The creak of the back door silenced them both. "Don't mention it to your mother," Dad said, his voice low. "Amy has hurt her enough."

"Forgot we're out of detergent," Mom said from the kitchen, her voice muffled by the wall separating the two rooms. "We'd better run to the store, Harold. I need to do one more load tonight." She appeared in the hallway, looking pretty in a light purple dress with the pearls Dad had bought her for their thirtieth wedding anniversary strung around her neck. She paused, eyes darkening. "Oh."

"Happy birthday, Mom." Taylor lurched forward, holding out the present like a peace offering.

She took it from him reluctantly, her brow lowering in a scowl. "Party ended a half hour ago."

Don't flip out, Taylor coached himself. *Not on her birthday.* He caught his dad's pleading look and gave the barest of nods. "I'm sorry I couldn't get here in time," Taylor said.

Mom grunted, sinking into the love seat next to Dad's recliner. Taylor slowly lowered himself to the couch across from them.

"So, who needed help this time?" Mom said.

The frustration welled up in Taylor, but he forced it back. "A friend."

"Did some firefighter guilt you into taking his shift?" Mom prodded. "Or were you just extra busy?"

The shift had been relatively uneventful, with only one small blaze that had easily been contained. Nothing like the blaze Taylor had encountered on his first day at the station. He'd grown bored with his job as a high adventure tour guide and picked firefighting as a second career. Eighteen months later and he still thought about that first blaze all the time. He could still see the horrified look on that woman's face when he told her she was now a widow. Her pink scrubs had looked almost orange in the fire's glow, a pinprick of light against the dark of the blacktop road as she fell to her knees and sobbed.

Taylor cleared his throat. "I'm sorry. I would've still made it on time, but I ran into a situation that I had to take care of."

Mom threw up her hands, the present still sitting untouched on her lap. "It's always something, Taylor."

He stared at the orange shag carpet, focusing on the black fur wedged between the fibers from the family cat. He could tell her the truth and she'd stop giving him flak for being late. But it wasn't worth seeing the pain fill her eyes until it spilled over. "You're right. I'm sorry."

Mom sighed, picking up the box in her lap and carefully sliding a finger under the tape holding the wrapping paper in place. "You're here. That's the important thing. Now, what have you brought me?" She tore the paper away, her mouth falling open at the contents. "Taylor," she gasped.

"I found it on the internet," Taylor said. "Bought it from some guy in Canada."

Mom's eyes glistened with tears and she carefully pulled the porcelain figurine out of the box. "It's perfect. Thank you."

Taylor nodded, giving his mom a tight hug. She'd been searching antique shops for months in an effort to find the figurine and complete her collection. Hopefully it would make up for both her children missing the party.

"That's real thoughtful," Dad said, his voice gruff. "Now you'll be sure to make it to the barbecue on Memorial Day, right? That's less than two months away."

"I'll be here," Taylor assured his father. And with any luck, Amy would be, too—sober and clean.

"Will you be coming alone?" Mom asked.

Taylor rolled his eyes. He knew she wasn't talking about Amy. "Yes, it'll just be me."

The silence stretched between them, but Taylor didn't want to get into it. He definitely wouldn't tell his parents he'd spent the past two months being set up by a professional matchmaker. He'd only signed up with Toujour because Corey, his best friend at the station, had suggested they join together. Taylor figured it couldn't hurt to have an expert's opinion—he always picked women with more baggage than a Boeing 747. So far, he hadn't found anyone through Toujour that he wanted to date more than twice.

An hour later, Taylor escaped his parents. They offered him leftovers, but he declined—this craptastic day called for takeout from his favorite Italian restaurant. He walked in the door of his condo and dropped his duffel bag, letting out a groan of relief. He could collapse into bed right now and sleep for an entire day. But the smell of Vinny's sample platter convinced him to stay awake just a little longer.

The click of nails sounded across the laminate flooring, and Ember trotted into the room, her tongue wagging in excitement. Taylor set his takeout on the counter and dropped to his knee, chuckling as she licked his face. He rubbed the border collie behind her ears. "I missed you, too, girl," he said. She was the one person in his life who didn't judge him.

Ember let out a happy bark.

"I promise we'll do something fun over the next forty-eight hours, okay? It's supposed to be beautiful tomorrow. How does the park sound?"

Ember jumped up, letting out another bark.

"I agree," Taylor said. He'd planned on spending the day driving Amy back to San Diego. At least that was one good thing about her finding her own ride home.

Taylor ate his takeout while watching Ember play in the small fenced-in yard. His phone rang, and his stomach dropped. Surely Amy wasn't calling him from jail again. She couldn't have been home more than an hour.

But it was Toujour's number that flashed across the screen. Brooke must've found him another date.

"Hey," Taylor said, already heading back inside to the desktop computer he kept in the spare bedroom.

"Hi, Taylor. Are you busy, or is this a good time to talk?" Brooke asked.

"You caught me at a good time." Taylor wiggled the mouse to wake up the computer screen.

"Great. I have another match for you. She's available for a date Friday evening or anytime Saturday, if you'd like to meet her. I just sent an email over with her basic information."

"I'm opening my inbox now." Dread welled up inside Taylor. He'd been on five dates in the past two months, but hadn't clicked with any of the women. Maybe he should tell Corey he was on his own. Taylor wanted a girlfriend, sure. But this was painful.

"Her name is Kaitlynn Monroe. You two have a lot in common—she loves hiking and dogs, and is a really caring and compassion person. Her husband passed away a year and a half ago, but she's eager and excited to reenter the dating world."

Taylor clicked on the email. A widow? That sounded like way more baggage than he wanted to deal with, although it also meant she probably had more depth than most of the women he'd dated. His mind flicked back to the woman from his first fire. Had she started dating again?

"I was thinking bowling would be a nice date," Brooke continued. "It'll give you plenty of time to chat, and it's a relaxed and low-stress environment. You could grab dinner or dessert afterward if you feel things are going well, but all I've mentioned to her is bowling."

"I like bowling," Taylor said noncommittally, scrolling through Kaitlynn's profile. She was the same age as him, loved Italian food, and enjoyed cooking. Well, at least they had that in common. But the widow thing was more than he could handle. He'd tell Brooke he wasn't interested and to keep looking. Or maybe he'd just tell her he was done.

His hand froze as he scrolled down, revealing the picture of Kaitlynn. He leaned forward and squinted.

No way.

His mind flew back to pink scrubs and a sobbing woman. She'd been beautiful even then. The Kaitlynn in the photo wore the lightest touch of makeup, and her hair was pulled back in a ponytail just like she'd worn that night. Her eyes held the same sadness in their depths. He couldn't forget her face if he tried. She'd haunted his dreams for eighteen months.

"Taylor, are you still there?" Brooke asked.

"Yes, sorry."

In the dark, he'd assumed her hair was brown, but it actually held an auburn tint that fit her somehow. Same cheekbones, same oval face, same arched eyebrows. It had to be her. The timeline fit.

"Did you tell Kaitlynn about me?" he asked.

"Yes, I showed her your picture and we talked. She was really drawn to you."

Surely she'd recognized him. Maybe there was something she wanted to tell him and that's why she'd asked for the date. Maybe she simply wanted to spend a few hours in the company of someone who had also been present on that horrific night.

"Would Friday or Saturday be better for you?" Brooke continued. "Or are you not interested?"

"No, I'm definitely interested." That night had haunted him, too. "Let's say Friday night. Maybe seven-thirty?"

"Excellent," Brooke said. "I'll confirm the details with Kaitlynn and get back to you tomorrow afternoon at the latest."

Taylor said goodbye and hung up the phone, still reeling. He'd thought about Kaitlynn a thousand times since that night. He'd wondered how she was doing, if she really had no friends or family to help her through the grief.

And now he would get to meet her. On a date.

Chapter Four

Kate could totally do this.

She closed her eyes, taking a deep breath. Her forehead rested lightly on hands that clutched the cool leather of the steering wheel. Air from the vents blew toward her, fanning hair away from her face.

She'd arrived at the bowling alley twenty minutes early, years of punctuality an unbreakable habit even in the face of stress. But she hadn't been able to force herself out of the car.

It's just a date, she reminded herself. *Nothing has to come from it. But it's good to get back out there.* That's all she needed from tonight—an easy, uneventful foray back into the dating world.

She focused on her breathing, forcing air in through her nose and out through her mouth in slow, even pulses, just like she coached frighten patients on the verge of hyperventilating.

You can do this, Kate.

"I can do this," she said aloud. She raised her head and forced herself to look at the building. It was fairly standard—stacked cinder block painted a deep blue. She could just make out the logo on the front door, which advertised laser tag, miniature golf, and bowling. A bright neon sign hung on one of the windowless walls. Just a bowling alley, like the half a dozen other bowling alleys she'd been to her in lifetime.

Slowly, Kate removed her keys from the ignition. The car would quickly fill with heat now that the A/C was off, even if it was only early April—a good incentive to get out of the car and walk inside. If she didn't go now, she'd be late, and that was an impression she didn't want to make. Taylor might be the type who was easily annoyed by tardiness. Her first date in eight years would be awkward enough without the silent treatment added in.

She flipped down the sun visor and glanced at her reflection in the small mirror. The makeup Liza had convinced her to buy looked nice—subtle, but still there. Liza had urged Kate to go with darker eyeshadows and a red lipstick, but Kate had uncharacteristically stood her ground and gone with more nude shades. She hadn't worn makeup since the first year of her marriage, and she would never make it through the date if she felt that self-conscious in her own skin. Best to ease back into things slowly, so hopefully the changes would stick.

Kate opened the door and placed one foot on the pavement. She'd balked at the price of the shoes—

nearly fifty dollars—but Liza had assured her the colorful wedge sandals, which made her calves look amazing and made Kate want to stand tall, were a steal. They were way outside Kate's comfort zone of flip-flops on her days off and comfortable tennis shoes for work, but she figured since she'd played it safe with the makeup, she could afford to take a risk on footwear, even if she'd spend most of the night in ugly bowling shoes.

She took a deep breath, then placed her weight on the sandals and stood, her feet protesting at the unfamiliar heels. She brushed invisible lint away from her new flowy white blouse. Her brand new jeans fit like a glove, the fabric softer against her skin than she'd known denim could be.

Kate gave the car one last fleeting look then locked the door, looping her purse over one shoulder. Hopefully Taylor wouldn't be able to tell every item of apparel she wore was new. Liza had assured her men never noticed those types of things, but Kate didn't want to look like she was trying too hard—or not hard enough. She was second-guessing everything.

Beau would've hated the jeans, hated the sandals, and hated the blouse. He would've criticized everything about her appearance, from the way she'd teased her hair to the silver hooped earrings that had been a high school graduation present from her grandfather.

The cool air of the bowling alley and scent of greasy pizza and nachos blasted Kate in the face. The loud beat of the music vibrated her bones, along with the loud *clack* of bowling balls hitting pins. Kate shrank back against the door, wishing more than anything she was home in her pajamas.

And then she saw him. His head was turned away from her as he watched a little girl enthusiastically push a bowling ball down a ball roller. Taylor wore a light blue button-down shirt with the sleeves rolled up to just below his elbows and dark blue denim jeans that hugged his hips. His gelled hair was a dark brown, the color similar to that of her morning coffee. Why was there something so familiar about his profile? He was more built than in his photo. She took a step forward, then hesitated.

Maybe it wasn't Taylor. His face was mostly hidden, and his profile could belong to any number of handsome men—strong jaw, prominent nose, nice cheekbones. He probably only seemed familiar because he looked so similar to Hollywood heroes in romantic comedies. Maybe it was a different man, waiting for a different date. If she went forward and introduced herself, only to find out it wasn't him, she'd die of embarrassment.

She reached back with her hand, feeling for the straight push bar on the door behind her. He wasn't here. She should leave. The only thing worse than going on her first date in eight years would be getting stood up on it.

The man turned, and his eyes locked onto hers, eyebrows lifting in recognition. Definitely Taylor. He waved a hand in acknowledgment and took a step forward. There was something about his eyes that stirred memories deep inside her.

She couldn't walk away now, no matter how much she regretted this date. Kate forced herself across the black carpet with bright neon designs, heart pounding in her chest. She could do hard things. This date was the right choice for her. She imagined herself shoving Beau's snarling voice into a dark corner of her mind and locking it away. He wouldn't ruin this for her.

"Hi," Taylor said, giving her a full smile of sparkling white teeth that had her stomach doing somersaults. He stuck out a hand. "It's nice to meet you, Kaitlynn."

Kate. I go by Kate. But she shook his hand and kept silent. No need to rock the boat in the first five seconds. "It's nice to meet you, too."

"I've already got lane seventeen reserved. We just need to grab our shoes."

"Okay." Kate fell into step beside Taylor, struggling to relax. She was on a date. Giddiness warred with nausea.

They grabbed shoes from the attendant and Taylor led her to their lane, where Kate pulled a pair of socks out of her purse and they both started slipping on their shoes. Kate was overly conscious of her every movement, aware of the man sitting beside her. Taylor seemed nice so far, and his casual attire made her feel better about her own clothing choices. Maybe this wouldn't be awful after all.

She was on a date. An actual, honest-to-goodness date.

Taylor's skin was tanned, veins and sinews popping in his hands as he finished tying his shoe. So different from the pasty-white complexion and slightly doughy appearance Beau had always sported.

"Are you a fan of bowling?" Taylor asked.

Kate jerked her gaze upward, feeling a blush work its way into her cheeks. She'd been staring like a high schooler on her first date. "It's been a few years since I've played," Kate said, skirting the question. "I'm only an amateur."

Taylor grinned, making heat flash through her.

"Excellent," he said. "I was worried I'd be embarrassed when you were this bowling pro and I barely manage a spare every third turn."

"It seems like we're evenly matched." The words registered half a second after they left her mouth, and her face burned. "I didn't mean . . ."

Taylor laughed, waving it aside. "I knew what you meant. So, how've you been?"

Kate squinted, the feeling of familiarity sweeping over her again. It'd been so long since she'd been on a first date that she couldn't remember if this was a typical conversation. "Um . . . Good, I guess."

"Good." Taylor nodded, as though genuinely relieved by her answer. "That's great. I've always wondered."

Her stomach rumbled with nerves while her palms grew clammy. Something was very wrong with this date. "I'm sorry," Kate said, the words taking all her courage. "Do we know each other?"

Taylor's eyes widened, making her stomach tremble even more. "You mean you don't recognize me?"

Something about his eyes pulled at her, but she couldn't place them. She was usually really good with names and faces, but his alluded her. Her first date in eight years, and it was with someone she knew but couldn't remember. Panic clawed at her throat as she fought to keep her composure. The new variable that had been introduced to this equation had frayed her already raw nerves.

"You look familiar, but I thought you just had one of those faces," Kate said. "I'm really sorry . . ."

"Oh man." Taylor rubbed a hand over his strong jaw. "I don't know why I didn't think of this. I assumed you knew and were okay with it. I recognized you from your photo almost immediately."

Kate should've given in to her fear and never stepped foot outside of the car. This was beyond humiliating. Embarrassed tears prick at her eyes and she forced them back. "You'll have to forgive me. I don't usually forget people like this."

Taylor's smile turned pained. "We met the night of the fire."

The sounds of bowling balls smacking against pins dimmed as his blue shirt and jeans morphed into full fire gear, a hat and jacket obscuring most of his features. Bile rose in her throat and she clasped her hands together tightly to hide the shaking. Out of all the men she could've been matched with, Brooke had found the one Kate had never expected to see again.

She should've recognized him immediately. A wife shouldn't forget the face of the man who informed her she was a widow.

Her entire body grew flush with heat as her vision blurred. She swayed, the bowling shoes pinching her feet with the movement and bringing to mind the raw blister she'd had on her foot that night. Taylor quickly wrapped his hands around her forearms, steadying her.

"Are you okay?" he asked.

She collapsed into the swivel chair around the small bowling table, her legs wet noodles. All she'd wanted was one normal date, but the universe seemed determined to refuse her even that small request. Beau was probably laughing as he watched her suffer. Maybe he'd even orchestrated this whole thing. It would be just like him to make her miserable, even from the grave.

A bottle appeared on the table in front of her, and Kate looked up, blinking slowly.

"Drink," Taylor said, sliding into the chair across from her.

She hadn't even realized he'd left. She broke the seal and took a long, slow swallow, her mind whirling. Taylor had known who she was and still agreed to the date. Why?

"Thank you," Kate ground out as she screwed the lid back on the bottle. This had to be some kind of joke to him—a fulfillment of a morbid curiosity about what she'd gone through the past year and a half. But it wasn't a joke to her. It was her life.

"I thought you knew," Taylor said.

Kate let out a hollow laugh. "Not a clue."

"Oh." The word was filled with meanings she couldn't decipher. "So, uh, why did you agree to a date with me?"

The humiliating question made something inside of Kate snap. Taylor wasn't Beau. She didn't have to worry about going home to him every night and dealing with the silent treatment, or rage, or whatever else he wanted to deal her.

This was Taylor's fault, not hers. And for once in her life, she wasn't going to take the blame.

"I agreed to this date because Brooke matched us up," Kate said, the words icy. "The real question is, why did you agree to this date?"

"I wasn't going to. But when I recognized you, I thought maybe you wanted to talk and get some kind of closure."

He hadn't wanted to go out with her. The reality sliced through Kate, a sharp pain that had her inhaling.

"Okay then." She reached down, fumbling with the knot in her shoelace.

"Wait!" Taylor ran a hand through his hair. "Geez, Kaitlynn. That came out all wrong."

"It's Kate," she spit out. This evening was nothing more than an opportunity for him to drag out painful memories of her past. She couldn't believe someone would be so cruel.

"Kate, then. That came out all wrong. I'll admit, the widow thing made me nervous when Brooke first called. It seemed like a lot."

"Yeah, it's been hard for me, too."

Taylor flushed, his dark skin pinking. "Crap, I keep screwing this up. I was going to say no, but then I recognized you, and I thought maybe you wanted to talk about it. I thought I owed it to you to show up, if that's what you needed."

"You don't owe me anything." Kate tore the knot free and flipped her hair over her shoulder, then started on the next knot. If he wanted to talk about that night, he'd gone out with the wrong person. She couldn't believe she'd wasted nearly a hundred dollars on an outfit for this.

"Please don't leave."

She wanted to leave more than anything. But if she walked out those doors, she didn't know if she'd ever be able to force herself back on another date. "Why?"

His sparkling blue eyes stared at her with worry and concern. "Because I've been a complete idiot, and I don't want things to end like this. You deserve better."

You deserve better. The words echoed in her mind, causing a lump to form in her throat. What a line.

She crossed her arms. "Do you have any idea how weird this is for me?"

He held his fingers up, a centimeter apart. "I have a very small idea."

"I've spent the past year and a half trying to put the past behind me. That night was one of the most traumatic of my life."

"No one would expect it to be anything less."

She wondered what Taylor would say if he knew the night wasn't traumatic for the reasons he probably thought it was. "I don't want to talk about that night."

"Okay."

"If that's why you came on this date, I'm leaving right now." She should leave anyway. But maybe she'd overreacted, and if she left now, she'd never go back.

"We don't have to talk about the fire."

"And I'm not talking about Beau. This isn't a chance for you to satiate your curiosity." Her heart hammered in her chest with the bold declarations, but it felt good to state an opinion and stick to it.

"Sounds fair."

She cocked her head, regarding Taylor. His eyes were open and vulnerable, his relaxed posture welcoming instead of threatening.

"This is really weird," she said.

"I know. Let me make it up to you."

Surely the date couldn't get any worse than this. If she stuck it out, she'd be able to move forward with the confidence that it could only go up from here. And she would've successfully taken that first, rocky step forward. Slowly, she nodded. "Okay."

He blew out a breath. "You'll stay, then?"

"I'll stay. But if you bring up Beau or the fire even once, I'm leaving."

"Deal."

She shifted from foot to foot, still not sure she'd made the right decision. Then she slowly bent down, allowing her hair to hide her expression as she retied her shoes with trembling hands.

I'm not doing this for him, she reminded herself. *I'm doing this for me. To prove I can.*

"I swear I'm not usually such an idiot," Taylor said.

Kate picked up her bowling ball, ignoring the comment. "I'm up first, right?"

Taylor folded his arms, regarding her. "Yes."

Kate took her place at the front of the line, eying the pins at the end. How had Beau managed to ruin her first date when he wasn't even alive? She would never be free of that man.

Just get through tonight, she told herself.

Kate let the ball fly. It swerved abruptly to the left, dropping into the gutter and making its way to the end of the lane. Her face heated, and knew she was blushing again. Why did she have to be born with red hair and fair skin? It always gave away her emotions.

She turned around, prepared to face whatever smug satisfaction or criticism Taylor had to dish out. He leaned forward, arms on the table, still regarding her with intense blue eyes.

"Good try," he said.

Kate let out a nervous laugh. "That was awful."

"Nah, it's just been a while. You need to warm up a bit."

Kate nodded and swallowed. She took her position again and took a deep breath, then let the ball roll. It hit slightly off center, taking down all but two pins.

"Great job!" Taylor held up his hand and Kate shyly gave him a high-five.

"Thanks." Kate held his gaze briefly before looking away. She hoped he knew she meant for more than bowling. She was so grateful he was playing it cool, not making a big deal over what had happened. Hopefully it lasted for the remainder of the date.

He smiled again—a look she was quickly realizing was a trademark of his. "You're welcome."

Chapter Five

She hadn't known. Taylor felt like an idiot for not immediately suspecting as much. It had been dark that night, the hazy smoke further distorting vision. He'd been suited up in his full gear, helmet and all, and his face had probably been streaked with ash and sweat from helping put out the blaze. She'd just found out her husband was dead and had been in shock, shaking despite the warm California air and the three blankets wrapped around her shoulders.

Of course she wouldn't remember him. Some people remembered traumatic events in crystal-clear intensity, like an instant replay every time the event came to mind. And some barely remembered it at all. He'd only lost three people to fires over the past eighteen months, but he remembered each event with near perfect detail. He shouldn't have assumed it'd be the same for the loved ones affected.

His phone buzzed, and he quickly opened and read the text. Amy was going off on one of her rants again.

Kate lined up the ball, then let it fly down the alley. It veered sharply to the left, but still managed to take down about half the pins. Taylor watched her shoulder slump before straightening again. When she turned to face him, she had a smile pasted on her lips. "I'd say I'm out of practice, but I've never been that great at bowling."

It seemed she had a decided lack of self-confidence as well. Taylor swallowed, his overprotective hero complex kicking into gear. Of course she'd taken an emotional beating these last eighteen months. That didn't mean he needed to fix it.

Taylor rose, grabbing his own bowling ball from the stand. "I've never been that great at bowling either, but I still enjoy the occasional game." He let his own ball fly, taking down about the same number of pins as she had. "I'm almost as good as you are."

Kate cocked her head to the side, as though trying to figure him out. Was she comparing him to her late husband, perhaps? He'd never dated a widow. Didn't want to date someone with that heavy of baggage. He should've let her leave, but he hadn't been able to let her walk out thinking badly of him.

He watched as she bowled another frame. The silence between them had passed uncomfortable ten minutes ago. Her deep auburn curls bounced against her back with the movement, her frame so slender as to be almost sickly.

He'd been the one to find Beau's body, and a death at his first fire had shook him. He could only imagine the kind of trauma Kate had experienced. He would make this date a good one. Then he would leave her life for good.

"So, Kate, tell me about your job. Your file said you're a nurse?" He'd guessed she was something medical from her scrubs the night of the fire.

"Yes. I used to work at the hospital in labor and delivery, but after . . ." She cleared her throat, twisting the bowling ball around in her hands until she found the finger holds. "Anyway, I'm at a pediatrician's office now." She let the ball roll and this time it hit dead-center, knocking down every pin.

"And you said you weren't a great bowler. I haven't managed to get a strike yet. Great job!" Taylor held up his hand for a high-five, and Kate tapped it with her own.

"Dumb luck, I guess."

"Nah, I think you've got hidden skills that are finally being set loose. So a labor and delivery nurse, and now a pediatrician's office. You must really like kids."

"I do."

Taylor tossed his ball down the lane, not caring when it headed straight for the gutter. "Do you have any nieces or nephews?" He remembered the way she'd shook her head and said there was no one she could call after that fire. He hadn't been able to get it out of his head for days.

"It's just me." Kate took a sip of her water and shrugged. "My grandpa and grandma raised me. They've both been gone over a decade now. I think my dad's still in prison. I'm not sure where my mom is, or if I have any siblings. Not exactly an ideal family, huh?"

"I'm so sorry." His phone buzzed again, but Taylor ignored it. Kate hadn't been exaggerating when she claimed to have no one. Had she at least had good insurance to help with the financial blow, or had she truly lost everything? He wanted to ask so badly but wouldn't go back on his promise.

Kate shrugged, the movement slow and a little self-conscious. "What about you?"

"What about me?"

"Do you have any nieces or nephews?"

"No, thank heaven." Taylor rolled the ball in his hands, then let it fly. Amy could barely take care of herself. He itched to check his phone, but didn't want Kate to think him rude. Hopefully Amy hadn't been picked up for a DUI. Her license had already been suspended, but he knew she still drove when she could get access to a car. He was already mentally rearranging his finances to help her post bail.

"Oh." Kate opened her mouth as though to ask a follow-up question, then pursed her lips and bowled her frame.

This date had entered painful territory.

"Tell me more about you," Taylor said. "What's your favorite thing to do on your day off?"

"I usually just run errands."

This conversation would need the jaws of life to recover. "Yeah, me too. I'm at work a lot, and when I'm not on shift I'm catching up on sleep and household stuff. There's a lot of down time at the station, or shifts when all we do is train, but on days when there are blazes . . ." He trailed off, realizing they were heading in a direction she'd asked the conversation not to go.

Kate sighed, twirling the ball between her palms. "It's weird not talking about it, isn't it?"

"A little." She wasn't shying away from the topic, and that somehow made her more attractive. "But that's okay. I don't want to do anything that would make you uncomfortable."

Kate looked up at the score board. "Last frame."

"Yup, and we're tied."

Kate chewed on her lip, then nodded, as though making a decision. She let the ball fly. It went straight and true, hitting the pins dead center and knocking them all down.

Taylor lifted his hands up in the air in a victory cry. "Strike! That was amazing, Kate. Good job."

She looked down, blushing. "I'm sure you'll get a strike, too."

"No way. You're totally going to win. You get to go again."

Kate rolled a gutter ball, then hit two pins on her last bowl. When she turned back around, her face was bright red. "Told you I suck."

"Even pros have off days." Taylor took his place and ended up with eight pins down. The pins on the score board danced in celebration, proclaiming Kate's win.

"Sorry I beat you," Kate said, sitting down and slipping off her shoes.

"Why? You earned that, fair and square. I think that means I owe you dinner."

"You don't need to do that."

"I want to," Taylor said, already cursing himself for asking her. Conversation had been stilted and uncomfortable. Why had he just asked for another hour of the same?

His phone buzzed again. Amy was getting more impatient.

He should leave Kate well enough alone. But she was a mystery he was dying to uncover.

Kate cocked her head to the side, as though regarding him, then finally nodded. "Okay. Dinner would be nice. Thank you."

Relief and disappointment hit him simultaneously. He wanted to get to know Kate better. But he wasn't equipped to deal with her past. He motioned to the Mexican restaurant connected to the bowling alley. It wasn't one of his favorites—he'd always opt Vinny's when given a choice—but it was close and the cafeteria-style line lent a casual atmosphere a sit-down restaurant wouldn't provide. "How's this?"

"Sounds great."

Kate followed him into the restaurant and stood silently beside him as they waited in line. Smoke billowed from a stove in the back and an employee let out a yelp.

"Everything okay?" Taylor asked the server, motioning to the stove.

The girl laughed. "Oh, yeah. Just training someone new. What can I get you?"

"A beef burrito, smothered with everything," Taylor said.

The girl quickly prepared the burrito, then looked up at Kate. "And what about you?"

Kate pointed to the sweet pork. "Is the sweet pork burrito peanut free?"

The employee nodded. "We're a nut-free restaurant."

"Okay then. I'll have that."

"You're allergic to nuts?" Taylor asked.

"Just peanuts. I always carry an epi-pen in my purse, just in case."

"That sucks. I love peanuts, especially on ice cream."

She shrugged. "The side effect of not breathing has kind of turned me off them."

A laugh rumbled in Taylor's stomach. He paid for their food, then took their tray to a table. More steam billowed up from the stove. Looked like their new employee wasn't suited for the kitchen.

"I can't stop thinking about it," Kate murmured as she cut her burrito. "You were there."

Taylor pushed the button on the side of his phone to silence another vibration. "I don't want to make you feel uncomfortable."

"I don't talk about it often. Aside from Liza, no one has ever asked me for details about that night."

Taylor set down his fork. "I'm so sorry, Kate. I'm sorry about your husband's death, and I'm sorry you didn't realize who I was before agreeing to this date." But he was beyond impressed with how she'd handled herself this evening. If he'd been in her situation, he wasn't so sure he would've stayed.

"It's not your fault." She dragged her fork through the spicy sauce smothering the top of her burrito. "I must've told Beau a thousand times to not smoke in the house, but he never listened."

"I saw the fire inspector's report. I hope that insurance didn't contest it."

"They did, for a while. But eventually we got everything straightened out. I moved into the new house about four months ago. It's really nice." She gave a small smile. "The fire wasn't all bad."

Taylor felt his eyebrows skyrocket in surprise, and he quickly took a bite of his taco salad to hide his shock. "A new house hardly makes up for the death of a husband."

"Everything happens for a reason."

What did that mean?

"I saw on your profile that you enjoy hiking," Kate said, changing the subject. "Me too, but it's been a few years since I've had a chance to do any. Are there any nearby trails I should try out?"

"There's this one that leads to a waterfall you've gotta try. Here, let me show you on a map." He pulled out his phone and showed her where the trail began, still trying to figure out what she'd meant.

His phone rang, the shrill sound making Kate jump.

"Sorry," Taylor muttered. Amy was getting more persistent. If he didn't answer, she'd just keep calling. "I've got to get this. Just a sec."

Kate nodded, glancing away to give him privacy. Taylor quickly answered the phone.

"Why have you been ignoring me?" Amy demanded.

"I've been busy," Taylor said, lowering his voice. Kate remained focused on her burrito. "What's up?"

"They're kicking me out if I don't pay my rent by five o'clock," Amy said. "I'm starting a new job next week and I swear I'm good for the money, if you can just lend it to me."

Taylor ran a hand through his hair and sighed. At least she hadn't been arrested. "How far behind are you?"

"Three months. But if I give them a couple thousand today, I think they'll lay off."

"That's a lot of money, Amy."

Kate let out a tiny cough. Taylor looked up, and she mouthed *sorry*, her cheeks bright red.

Taylor stared. He barely noted the hazy air around Kate before an ear-splitting shriek filled the restaurant. Flames flew up from the grill top and Taylor jumped to his feet, shoving the phone in his pocket without even turning it off.

"Everyone out!" he yelled, heading toward the kitchen.

Patrons jumped to their feet, rushing toward the door. Taylor caught a glimpse of Kate's red hair in the crowd as he fought his way toward the kitchen. The flames were three feet high, nearly brushing the ceiling.

He saw a pimply employee grab a pan of water out of the sink.

"Don't!" Taylor shouted. He reached around the flames, quickly flicking off the burner.

"I don't know what happened," the kid wailed, his voice raising an octave in fear.

"Get the fire extinguisher," Taylor yelled. He grabbed a frying pan and tossed it on top of the flames. Orange glowed underneath it, the angle of the handle not allowing the oxygen to be smothered completely.

Taylor glanced around and saw a box of baking soda next to a mixer. He grabbed the pan off and sprinkled the baking soda over the flames, further cooling them.

"Here." The boy shoved a fire extinguisher into Taylor's hands.

Taylor instantly doused the stove in foamy sodium bicarbonate, not stopping until the extinguisher sputtered and stopped. He handed it over to the kid, feeling his heart rate slow. "There."

And that's when the overhead sprinklers flicked on, dousing them in water. Taylor flinched as the cold drops soaked his clothes. When was the last time they'd had this place inspected? He flicked the water out of his eyes. "Your sprinkler system is faulty. This entire building could've been in flames by now."

"I don't know what happened," the boy said, his voice continuing to rise. "One second everything was fine, and the next the stove was on fire."

Taylor heard the wail of sirens in the distance and rolled his eyes. Station forty-one was always so slow to respond.

"It's called a grease fire." Taylor clapped the boy on the back. "Never try to put one out with water. Could've happened to anyone. You got lucky this time."

A firefighter raced into the building, and Taylor briefed him on the situation.

"We've got it from here," the firefighter said, brushing past Taylor.

Taylor stood there for a moment, feeling useless. He pulled his phone out of his pocket, the screen dark and device dripping in water. Amy was going to be pissed.

Wait. Where was Kate?

Taylor raced from the restaurant, frantically looking around the parking lot. But Kate was gone.

Chapter Six

Kate stood under the scalding hot water, shivers still wracking her body. That fire alarm had gone off, and suddenly she'd been pulling into her driveway with no memory of how she'd gotten there.

She couldn't believe she'd ditched Taylor. How embarrassing.

Eventually she warmed up and crawled between her crisp sage green sheets. She stared at the white ceiling shadowed by moonlight, willing her muscles to relax and mind to slow so she could sleep. The bed felt blessedly empty and spacious without Beau's large frame taking his half out of the middle. She'd had to buy a new mattress after the fire, and she'd picked one soft as a cloud—six years of sleeping on a hard-as-a-rock mattress for Beau's back was long enough.

Beau. She rested a hand on her forehead, staring at the textured ceiling. That fire alarm had gone off and her instincts had taken over. But Beau hadn't been able to run away. He'd barely been able to limp. Had he realized what was happening before passing out, or had he simply gone from sleeping to dead? She hoped he hadn't suffered.

She couldn't believe she'd actually gone on a date with someone who wasn't him. Taylor had been so different—tall and strong, kind and considerate. The date had been beyond awkward—and now she was beyond humiliated—but Taylor had tried to fill the awkward silences with kind conversation. Beau had been that way before the accident, too. Six unimaginably difficult years had dulled his better qualities, but they had been there.

A tear slipped out of the corner of Kate's eye, and she wiped it away. She didn't miss the Beau she'd lived with for most of their marriage. But she desperately missed the Beau from their courtship, the one who had tenderly kissed her forehead and brought flowers to the hospital to brighten her day. She'd been so optimistic on the day they wed. The ceremony had been simple, just ten minutes at the courthouse with a clerk standing nearby as the witness. But it had been the happiest moment of her life.

Then, scarcely before the ink was dry, Beau had broken his back. After rehab he'd started drinking to dull the pain. It had turned him into someone she didn't even recognize.

Kate rolled onto her side, letting tears leak onto her pillow. She didn't want to date a handsome fireman who made her stomach flip and cheeks heat. She wanted to be a wife in a comfortable, loving marriage. One where she was a partner and not a doormat. Where she could trust her husband to weather life's difficulties with kindness.

Taylor had looked at her with such unmasked pity when he realized she hadn't known who he was. All in all, her first foray back into the dating world couldn't have been more of a disaster.

Kate spent the rest of the weekend cleaning her house and running errands. She even managed to fit in a short hike, taking one of the trails Taylor suggested. When she walked into work on Monday morning, she felt groggy and exhausted. She dropped her purse in the bottom drawer of her desk, then booted up the computer to pull patient charts.

"How'd it go?"

Kate jumped at Liza's voice. She swiveled in the chair to look up at her friend's eager face. "Fine."

Liza frowned, sinking into the chair next to Kate's. "That doesn't sound very convincing."

The humiliating and uncomfortable date washed over Kate once again. She didn't want to talk about this, especially not to her one and only friend. "I don't think we'll go out again," Kate said simply.

"Uh-oh. He didn't treat you badly, did he?"

"No, Taylor was a perfect gentleman."

"Did he have bad breath?"

"No."

"Was he really arrogant and it wasn't fun to bowl with him?"

"No."

"Was he shorter than you?"

A smile cracked the corner of Kate's mouth. "No."

"Then what's the problem?"

The problem was he was too handsome, too kind, and too considerate. And had too many connections to the past she was trying to leave behind. "I didn't feel a connection," Kate said, deciding vague was the best way to approach this.

"Give it a little time." Liza rubbed a comforting hand up and down Kate's arm. "The first date was bound to be difficult. How are you doing? I imagine it was a really hard night for you."

Yes, but not for the reasons Liza assumed. "I'm doing okay."

"Well, keep at it. No one expects you to fall in love with the first guy you date. I'm really proud of you for getting back out there, Kate. I don't know if I'd be as brave as you if the situation was reversed."

Brave. Kate inwardly laughed. That was the exact opposite of what she felt. Cowardly was a much better word. If she'd been brave, she would've insisted she and Beau go to counseling, that he go to AA meetings, asked for a divorce—anything but stay in an unhealthy relationship and wither into nothing.

The day was busy, and Kate thankfully didn't have a moment to spare discussing her date with Liza. She rushed out of the clinic nearly thirty minutes late and sped to Toujour for her appointment with Brooke.

Kate had barely sat down in one of the Parlours when Brooke breezed into the room, looking put-together and chic in a plum-colored skirt and white blouse. Kate looked down at her wrinkled Mickey Mouse scrubs, biting her lip.

"Sorry I'm late," Kate said quickly. "Work was really crazy today."

Brooke sank gracefully into a chair, waving away the words with a flick of her wrist. "Don't worry about it. So, how did your date go with Taylor?"

Kate shifted in her seat, looking down at her hands. "He was very kind," she said diplomatically.

"Kate."

Kate looked up, surprised at the use of her nickname.

Brooke smiled. "Taylor told me you preferred that to Kaitlynn."

"Yeah," Kate said.

"He also told me what happened."

Tears pooled in Kate's eyes, and she blinked quickly, fighting them back. "I kept thinking he looked familiar, but couldn't place where I'd seen him. I thought he just had one of those faces."

"I am so incredibly sorry. I can't even begin to imagine how traumatic that must've been for you. That is not what I ever wanted for you, much less on your very first date."

Kate would not let the tears fall. "It's okay. It's my fault, really. I should've recognized him. If I'd realized who he was, I wouldn't have agreed to a date. I think I placed Taylor in an uncomfortable situation. I feel really bad about that."

"He was worried when he couldn't find you after the restaurant fire."

Kate stared at her chipped nails. "I'm so embarrassed about that. I overreacted."

"I think Taylor understands." Brooke flipped open the lid on her laptop. "Now, let's get into the nitty gritty. How would you rate Taylor's attractiveness, on a scale of one to ten? I know this is a silly question, but physical attraction is important in a relationship, and if it's not there, it usually means the relationship won't work out."

Kate felt her face flush red and bit her lip. "I guess a seven or eight." *Liar,* her mind shouted. He was a solid ten at least.

Brooke's eyebrow raised, but she quickly pulled her face into a blank expression. "That's not bad for our first try. Can you tell me a little bit about how the date went, in your own words?"

Kate picked at a loose thread on her scrub top. "Taylor was very kind. It only took a few minutes for me to figure out who he was. He thought I wanted to go on the date to discuss that night. When he realized that wasn't the case, he was very respectful and didn't push me."

"Taylor is a considerate person," Brooke said. "It's something his dates always comment on, and one of the reasons I matched the two of you up. How did the date progress from there?"

"We bowled. We talked about our likes and dislikes. He invited me to dinner, and I agreed." She still wasn't sure why. She should've left the second she realized who he was. "It was uncomfortable but okay until the fire alarm."

They talked for a few more minutes, and Kate gradually loosened up, becoming a little freer with her answers.

Brooke finally shut the lid of her laptop and leaned forward. "Taylor felt awful about how the date started off, but he really enjoyed spending time with you. I know that, given the circumstances, you might never want to see Taylor again. I think he's aware of that as well. But he had a really good time, and he wants a second date."

Kate's stomach swooped, and she pressed her lips together in a tight line. "He said that?"

"Yes."

A pity date. What other explanation could there be? She'd left in the middle of their date without so much as a goodbye, for crying out loud. For a moment, she pictured the way his baby blues had burned into her soul.

No. She did not need a pity date.

"He shouldn't feel obligated to take me out again because of the circumstances," Kate said.

"Taylor and I talked about that. I really don't think that's his motive. He likes you, Kate. He loved discussing hiking with you. He admired the way you handled the situation and appreciated your sense of humor."

Sense of humor? Nothing about that date had been even close to funny.

"He wants to explore and see where this could go," Brooke finished.

The old Kate—the Kate who had put up with Beau's abuse for six years—would agree to the date out of obligation and a desire to not hurt Taylor's feelings. She opened her mouth, *yes* on the tip of her tongue.

But she'd come to Toujour to change her old ways and find lasting happiness.

"I don't know if I want to go out with him again," Kate said slowly.

She expected Brooke to argue with her. To insist she and Taylor were a perfect match. But Brooke just nodded and said, "I understand completely."

"It's not that he wasn't nice. He was."

"Kate." Brooke rested a gentle hand on her knee. "I understand. And so will Taylor."

"He seems like a great guy. It's just too much right now."

"Let's not say no, then. Let's say not right now." Brooke flipped her laptop open again. "In case you didn't want to go out with him again immediately, I found a few more matches you might be interested in, as well as the two I showed you before. How about I set you up on dates with a couple of those men, and we can revisit whether or not you want to go out with Taylor again later?"

"Okay," Kate said.

But she wouldn't go out with him again. The new Kate was no one's damsel in distress.

Chapter Seven

Taylor spent the rest of the weekend in San Diego, trying to get the situation with Amy under control. The landlord had agreed to give Amy some time to come up with the rest of the cash if Taylor paid half the back rent immediately. In the end he caved. Amy needed him. She needed support and encouragement. If she had someone to look after her, he knew she'd improve.

And the San Diego Fire Department happened to have an opening.

On Monday morning he hung up the phone, not at all surprised that Kate didn't want another date. It wasn't like it had gone especially well, and his connection to her past had no doubt rattled her. What did surprise him was how much the realization he'd most likely never see Kate again disappointed him.

Tuesday morning, Taylor rolled out of bed at four-thirty and was to the fire station in time for his five a.m. shift. His best friend, Corey, was already in the kitchen, preparing breakfast casseroles for the guys. His dark hair was messy, the apron barely fitting around his muscled torso.

"Hey man," Corey said, giving a head nod. "How was your weekend?"

"Unexpected and bizarre." Taylor washed his hands in the sink, then started cracking eggs in a bowl. It wasn't his turn for mess duty, but he didn't mind helping Corey out.

"What do you mean?" Corey asked.

"I went on a Toujour date."

"Oh yeah?" Corey raised an eyebrow. "I went on one, too. She was pretty cool, and we're going out again. I haven't had an awful date yet from them. What did you guys do that was so bizarre?"

"We went bowling. She beat me."

"I'm not surprised. You suck."

Taylor glared. "Not the point. The bizarre part was that I already knew her."

"An ex?" Corey winced sympathetically. "That blows. Didn't you recognize her from the photo?"

"Yes. But she isn't an ex, and she didn't recognize me."

"Okay . . ." Corey dumped the sausage into the frying pan and it sizzled, steam rising toward the oven hood. "Are you going to make me keep guessing, or are you just going to tell me?"

"Remember my first fire?"

Corey squinted. "Vaguely. A house fire, right? Guy died."

"Yes. And I told the widow."

"I kind of remember that. She was super hot."

"Yes." Taylor raised an eyebrow meaningfully.

Corey's eyes widened. "No."

"Yes."

"No!"

"When my matchmaker sent her profile over, I assumed Kate knew that I was the firefighter from that night and wanted closure or something. But she had no idea."

Corey let out a whistle. "Wow. Talk about a rocky start."

Taylor finished cracking eggs into the bowl and grabbed a whisk. "She was pissed at first. But then she relaxed, and she was pretty cool. Until a fire alarm went off."

Corey winced. "Ouch."

"Yeah. Grease fire in the kitchen. By the time I got it under control, she was gone. My matchmaker says Kate doesn't want to see me again."

"Can you blame her?"

Taylor grabbed the towel and flicked it at Corey, who jumped away, laughing.

"I'm just saying I can see where she's coming from," Corey said, and his smile faded. "That must've been really hard for her."

"Yeah." Taylor poured the eggs over the sausage, and Corey continued scrambling. "I really thought she knew, which I now realize makes me an idiot. But man, I can't get her out of my head. Then I had to go down to San Diego and help Amy out."

"She's drinking again?"

Taylor blew out a sigh. "Yeah, a lot. I'm thinking of moving down there to help her more."

Corey paused. "Wow, man. That's a big decision."

"I know. But she needs me."

Soon the kitchen was filled with laughter as they shared breakfast with the rest of the guys. They were just cleaning up when Glenn, one of the older firefighters, pulled Taylor to the side.

"What's up?" Taylor asked.

"I was hoping you'd do me a favor," Glenn said. "I'm supposed to go to that pediatric safety fair a week from Saturday with Corey, but my friend's selling tickets for that day to a play my wife really wants to see. Think you can cover for me?"

"Sure," Taylor said. The answer was automatic, and he did a mental flip through his calendar, hoping there wasn't something else he was supposed to do. "Just text me the information, and I'll do it." He'd never done a safety fair before, but it sounded fun.

"Thank you." Glenn clapped him on the shoulder. "Me and the missus really appreciate it. I can always count on you."

I can always count on you . . . Taylor almost snorted. His parents would laugh out loud if they heard someone saying that.

Amy called three more times that week. He spent the weekend in San Diego again, driving her to various job interviews while secretly wondering if his parents were right—he made things too easy for Amy. But when he saw her excitement at finally landing a job, he banished her parents voices from his mind. She needed someone to be in her corner.

As soon as Taylor got home, he filled out the job application for San Diego. Yet he couldn't bring himself to send it in. Even almost two weeks later, he couldn't stop thinking about Kate.

On Saturday morning, Taylor sat in the passenger's seat of one of the station's pumper trucks as Corey negotiated the ever-present Los Angeles traffic on their way to the pediatric safety fair.

"Thought any more about the San Diego job?" Corey asked, pulling Taylor out of his thoughts.

"Yeah," Taylor said. "It's just a lot, you know? I'd have to sell the condo, and Mom and Dad would be furious."

"That's a tough choice," Corey said.

Taylor couldn't agree more.

"Come over tonight. We'll watch the game and hang out."

"Nah," Taylor said. "Thanks for the offer, but I'm going to grab takeout and send in that application to San Diego. Who knows? I might not even get an interview."

"You will. If you change your mind, the offer stands."

"Thanks, man."

Corey made a wide turn into the parking lot of the three-story medical plaza. Taylor climbed out of the truck and straightened one of the suspenders that held up his turnout pants. A police cruiser already sat at the opposite end of the parking lot, and a Korean Barbecue food truck was firing up the grill. Taylor propped open the various doors on the side of the truck so the kids could see where they kept the hose, tools, and other equipment they used when fighting a blaze.

"Thank you so much for coming," came a soft voice from behind him—one that made Taylor freeze with his hand on a compartment latch. "The kids are really excited about meeting you. We've worked really hard to advertise this safety fair and hope to get a good turnout today."

Slowly, Taylor turned around. "Uh, hi, Kate."

She took a step back, her eyes widening. Her hair was pulled up high in a ponytail, loose curls tumbling down her back. Taylor itched to touch the silky strands, and he curled his fingers into his palms. Running his hands through her hair would be completely and totally inappropriate. She wore the barest trace of makeup, and her white scrub top with a Tinker Bell print looked better on her than it should. Those green scrub bottoms . . . well, he'd never realized they could showcase a woman's curves so well.

Taylor blinked, focusing on Kate's wide, green eyes.

"I didn't realize the safety fair would be where you work," he said.

"And I didn't realize you would be the firefighter sent. There's so many stations in L.A."

He grinned, hoping to put her at ease. "What are the odds, right? I wasn't supposed to come, but I took over for another guy at the last moment."

"Listen, about last week . . ."

He held up a hand, cutting her off abruptly. "You don't need to say anything. I understand. Really, I do."

Her shoulders straightened and she gave a brisk nod. "Well, thank you for coming. Basically we want the kids to ask questions, learn basic fire safety, and feel comfortable around firefighters so that if—heaven forbid—they are caught in a blaze, they won't hide from help." Her eyes clouded for a moment, but then she blinked, and it was gone.

Strike a Match

"Are you okay?" Taylor asked quietly.

"I'm fine." She opened her mouth as though to say something else, then shrugged. "I've got to go check on a few other things, but I'll be back before the fair starts in a half hour to help out at your station."

Taylor watched Kate walk away, his gaze lingering on her slender form as conflicting emotions blossomed inside him. What were the odds that out of all the pediatrician offices and firefighters in L.A., they'd end up here together?

"Wow," Corey said from behind Taylor. "If I'd known the nurses were so hot, I wouldn't have complained so much when the chief told me I'd drawn the short straw."

Taylor smacked Corey on the head, and he laughed, ducking. "That's Kate," Taylor said.

"Is that supposed to mean something to me?"

"The girl from Toujour."

Corey's eyes widened, and he whipped back to stare at her. "No way. The widow?"

"Yeah."

"You didn't mention she's at least an eight on the looks scale."

Kate was a ten if she was anything. "I feel awful." Taylor ran a hand through his hair and blew out a breath. "She doesn't want to see me."

"But you want to see her."

Taylor folded his arms, watching Kate as she spoke with the police officer across the parking lot. "She intrigues me."

"Dude, don't let your hero complex go into overdrive on this one."

"I don't know what you're talking about."

Corey snorted. "The widow who claimed to have no family and has been going it alone for the last year and a half? Come on—that's exactly the kind of train wreck you run right toward."

"I'm not running toward anything."

"Good." Corey clapped him on the back. "Toujour will find you someone perfect. Promise."

It was almost twenty minutes before Kate came back. Taylor watched as she spoke with the police officer, the cook at the food truck, the representative from the state advertising various services to help young parents. She seemed to always speak softly—people kept leaning forward to hear her—and the timid smile on her lips tugged at his heart. What had happened to this woman? After the way she'd yelled at him, he didn't believe she was simply shy.

Kate came back just as the first parents and their children arrived. "Sorry," she said.

"Hey, no problem." Taylor pulled a stack of pamphlets out of a box and handed half of them to Kate. "We're doing just fine over here."

"Okay." Kate smiled, her cheeks pink. She turned away from Taylor, focusing on the small child running toward her. The little boy plowed into her, making her stumble. Taylor put a hand on her back to steady her and Kate laughed, giving the boy a hug. "Hi, Eli."

"I can't believe it's finally here," he said. "I've been waiting forever." His eyes flicked toward Taylor, and Eli lowered his voice. "Is that a *real* fire fighter?"

"Yes he is. Eli, this is Firefighter Coleman."

Taylor crouched down, giving the little kid a high-five. He couldn't be more than six years old, and his eyes sparkled with delight. "Hi, Eli."

"I want to be a firefighter just like you when I grow up."

"That's a worthy career choice," Taylor said.

"Have you ever rescued someone from a burning building?"

Taylor glanced at Kate, who's lips were now pursed in a tight line. "Yes," Taylor said, rising to his feet. "How about I show you around the fire truck, Eli?"

For the next two hours, Taylor and Corey were flooded with eager kids, and Taylor started to go hoarse from all the talking. The crowd had finally died down when Kate appeared. She held a sandwich out to Taylor.

"Compliments of the doctors."

"Thanks." Taylor unwrapped the sub and took a big bite. "I'm starving."

Kate handed a sandwich to Corey as well, then took a smaller, more dainty bite of her own sandwich. "I tried out that trail you recommended. You were right—it was well-worth the hike."

"I'm glad you enjoyed it," Taylor said. Kate was being friendly and kind—did that mean she was rethinking her refusal for a second date?

"Kate!"

Taylor looked up to see a middle-aged woman in Disney princess scrubs striding across the parking lot.

"You need to get going, honey. You don't want to show up to your date in scrubs."

Taylor felt his stomach lurch. Kate flicked her gaze to him, then looked down at the ground. "I'd better go. It was nice to see you again, Taylor."

"You too," he muttered.

He watched her walk away, struggling to keep down the jealousy. Kate had certainly wasted no time in moving on to her next match. That was good. He wanted her to be happy. Besides, he was going to San Diego. A second date would've been pointless since he'd be moving soon. He'd email the application as soon as he grabbed Vinny's and got home.

Kate would be nothing but a distant memory in a week.

Chapter Eight

Kate looked up at the building, an upscale Italian restaurant named Vinny's with a Tuscany design. She'd only spent ten minutes in her car instead of twenty. That was quantifiable progress, and she'd take it.

It had taken all her courage to accept another date after the somewhat traumatic one with Taylor. But she'd agreed to go out with Randy, an accountant in his early forties with a five-year-old daughter. The age difference—and the child—made her nervous, but Brooke had convinced her to give Randy a shot.

Kate smoothed down her skirt, straightened her purse strap on her shoulder, then headed across the parking lot. The scent of garlic and cheese instantly soothed her nerves, and she took a deep breath. Whatever else tonight brought, at least she'd get a delicious Italian meal out of the deal.

"Hi," Kate told the hostess. "I'm meeting someone here. Randy?"

"Oh yes," the hostess said, tugging at the black vest hugging her chest. "Right this way, please. He asked to be seated immediately so he's already at a table."

Kate clutched her purse strap and followed the waitress to a quiet corner of the restaurant. A man with thinning hair and a hint of gray around the temples quickly rose, giving her a tentative smile.

"Kate?" he asked, extending a hand.

"Hi," she said, giving it a brief shake then sitting down. "It's nice to meet you, Randy."

"You as well."

Kate gave him an uncomfortable smile, then slowly picked up her menu. "Have you ever eaten here before?"

"No, but I've always wanted to. I knew Toujour could get us reservations for a Friday night."

Kate opened the menu, her mouth going slack. Their meal would cost him as much as she spent on a week of groceries.

"It smells delicious," Kate said. "I've always loved Italian food."

"Me too. My grandma emigrated from Italy when she was a teenager. I'm planning on taking my daughter there next summer on vacation. Have you ever been to Italy?"

"No." Kate had never been outside of California. Heck—she'd never even made it to the northern part of the state. Her parents had been too drunk or high to worry about vacations, and her grandparents had lived on a minuscule fixed income. But she'd love to travel someday. In the beginning, she'd thought maybe she and Beau would be able to save up and travel at least a little bit, just a weekend getaway or something, but there'd never been money to spare. He'd been unable to move around much anyway.

Taylor seemed like the type of guy who'd be up for any adventure. He'd probably traveled lots. Kate could almost imagine climbing to the top of a Hawaiian volcano with him, his easy smile make the ache in her muscles disappear.

"You'd love Italy," Randy said. "Everyone does. Greatest country in the world."

Kate blinked, quickly forcing thoughts of Taylor out of her mind and focusing on Randy. He deserved an attentive date.

"My daughter's really excited to visit," Randy continued. "It'll be just the two of us. We don't have family over there anymore—just distant cousins I've had next to no contact with—but it'll be great to visit the town where Nonna grew up."

Kate took a sip of her water, glancing at the menu. The chicken Alfredo and Tuscany lasagna were the least expensive items, within a dollar of each other. Should she go with the cheaper chicken Alfredo, or the slightly more expensive lasagna? She was more in the mood for something like the white wine truffle pasta, but the Alfredo was probably delicious, too. "Your daughter is five, right?"

"Just celebrated her birthday last month. Claire stays with me on the weekends, but her mother lives nearby and is good about letting me see Claire whenever I want. Our divorce was a mutual decision and we're pretty good friends now. We still take a family vacation together every summer."

"That's great," Kate said. Best friends with his ex? No thanks. She didn't want to get in the middle of that relationship. That was the nice thing about Taylor— there was no ex, no children to muddy the waters. But it was unfair to want someone without a past when she had so much of one herself. Taylor had flat-out said the widow thing freaked him out. She'd bet it freaked out a lot of other guys, too.

Stop thinking about him, she told herself. Sure, it had been pleasant spending time with him today. He was an excellent conversationalist, and watching him interact with the children had been heartwarming. But she couldn't reopen that door. It was too weird.

"What about you?" Randy asked.

"What about me?"

"Do you have any children?"

"Oh. No."

Randy nodded. "I just have Claire. Her mom and I divorced shortly after she was born, so I've never been as involved as I would've liked to be. Have you only been married the once?"

"Yes." Kate took another quick sip of her water. "My husband passed away eighteen months ago."

"My matchmaker mentioned that. I'm so sorry."

Kate forced a smile. "It's been challenging, but I'm ready to move forward with my life."

The waitress appeared then, a notepad and pen in her hand. "Hi, I'm Rosa," she said. "Do we want to start off with some drinks tonight?"

"We'll take a bottle of red wine for the table," Randy said.

Kate's stomach curled. Beau's substance abuse had turned her off alcohol forever. "Just a water for me."

Randy raised an eyebrow. "Red wine goes with everything. I'll make sure they bring us a good year."

Hadn't Randy read her profile, where she'd clearly stated she didn't drink? She could feel his annoyance rising, feel him pushing her to bend to his will. But she wouldn't relent on this. "No, thank you."

The waitress nodded. "Are you ready to order now, or should I give you a minute?"

"I'm ready," Kate said quickly. Maybe if she kept Rosa talking long enough, Randy would forget they'd ever been on the subject of alcohol, which inevitably led to the subject of Beau.

Randy looked surprised, but nodded. "Would you like me to order for you?"

Kate looked down at the menu. "I'm allergic to peanuts so I'd better order for myself."

"Okay," Randy said, his tone a little abrupt.

Kate didn't want to owe Randy anything, so she'd order the cheapest item on the menu. She pointed to the chicken Alfredo. "If I order this entree, will I be okay?" Sometimes they used peanut oil to fry the chicken.

"I believe that dish is nut-free, but let me double check with my manager." The waitress snagged a man in slacks and a button-down shirt as he walked past. "Thad, we've got a question for you."

The middle-aged man with a receding hairline smiled. "Of course. What can I help you with?"

The waitress pointed to the chicken Alfredo. "She's allergic to peanuts. Is this dish nut free?"

The manager nodded almost immediately. "Yes, that dish is safe." He took the menu from the waitress's hand and showed a different dish to Kate. In small script underneath the item it said *may contain nuts and milk*. "All our dishes with allergy concerns are labeled in the menu."

"Thank you," Kate said, feeling embarrassed. She should've noticed that herself—would've if the date hadn't flustered her.

"Of course. It's always best to double check." He turned to the waitress. "Make a note on the order, just to be extra sure."

The waitress nodded, and the manager left.

"Is that what you'd like, ma'am? The chicken Alfredo?"

"Yes," Kate said, handing the waitress her menu.

The waitress nodded, jotting down the order. "And what about you, sir?"

"I'll have the white wine truffle pasta."

Darn. Kate should've ordered that instead of worrying so much about the money. She could've at least gone for the lasagna. Randy had picked the restaurant—he obviously had enough money to cover the price.

They talked about Randy's daughter and what had brought them each to Toujour while waiting for their meals. Kate tried to keep her focus on the conversation, but her mind kept drifting to the way Taylor had looked in his fire suit mere hours earlier. She'd never realized how attractive suspenders could be. Had he already accepted another Toujour date? No doubt someone as attractive and kind as Taylor wouldn't stay on the market long.

"Here you go." Rosa set a steaming hot plate of food in front of each of them.

"Thank you," Kate murmured, inhaling deeply. Divine, even if it hadn't been her first choice.

Kate picked up her fork and dove in, barely withholding a moan of pleasure. She hadn't eaten this well in months. She never wasted money on takeout, and cooking for one was depressing. She resorted to a lot of TV dinners.

"Delicious," Randy said. "How's your food?"

"Excellent," Kate said. The front door swung open, sending a blast of warm air over the table. Kate looked up, then quickly did a double-take. Taylor spoke to the hostess, then took a seat on a bench. He looked up, as though sensing her gaze, and his eyes widened in surprise. He lifted a hand in a little wave.

Kate quickly looked down, taking another bite of her food. That cleft in his chin would be her undoing. If he was here on a date as well, she would die of awkwardness. Shouldn't Toujour pay attention to that sort of thing?

"I've always loved truffles," Randy said. "My ex is an excellent cook, and sometimes she invites me over for dinner when I take Claire home on Sundays."

Kate peeked another glance at Taylor. He still sat alone on the bench. She coughed, quickly looking away before he sensed her gaze. Another cough ripped through her. She hadn't expected the Alfredo to be spicy, but her tongue and mouth burned. She took another bite, then coughed again.

"Do you cook?" Randy asked.

"I can, but I don't especially enjoy it." Kate coughed again, putting a hand to her suddenly tight chest. Her vision grew fuzzy, and a sinking realization came over her.

Anaphylactic shock. There were peanuts in the dish.

Kate coughed again, her chest burning with the effort. She put a hand to her head, dizziness overwhelming her.

"Kate?" Randy's voice sounded far away and concerned.

"Can't . . . breathe . . ." Kate wheezed. She fumbled for her purse, knocking it underneath the table where the contents spilled everywhere. She coughed again, black spots dotting her vision as panic tore through her.

"You're really pale," Randy said. "What do I do?"

Kate tried to tell him to get her epi-pen, but couldn't get the words through her swollen lips. She slumped sideways in the booth, her head knocking against the wall as she attempted to lie down. Why hadn't Randy called 911?

Suddenly hands were underneath her knees, pulling until her legs dangled off the end of the bench and her head was flat against the cushion. "Do you have the epi-pen?" the voice said urgently. "Kate!"

Taylor. Relief swept through her, and she pointed limply to the floor.

"She started coughing, then went pale," Randy said, his voice high and squeaky. The hands left Kate's legs, and she was vaguely aware of Taylor crouched underneath the table, rifling through the contents of her purse.

"She's allergic to peanuts," Taylor said. "There must've been something in the dish. Found it."

Kate felt a sharp jab in her upper thigh, then hands gently rolled her onto her side. Kate gasped, struggling to stay conscious as her brain grew more deprived of oxygen. Was her epi-pen even current? She hadn't had a reaction in at least a few years, and couldn't remember the last time she'd filled the prescription. As she continued to struggle for breath, panic coursed through her. What if the pen was expired and wouldn't work? She knew all too well the dangerous effects of expired medications. How could she have been so stupid?

"She asked the waitress if there were peanuts, and she assured her there were not," Randy said, his voice turning hard and angry.

"Kate?" Taylor's face was close to hers, and his breath wafted over her like a cool breeze. "Kate, stay with me." His phone was to his ear. "Yes, I need an ambulance."

"What happened?" the frantic voice of the waitress asked. Kate looked up, taking in Rosa's panicked expression.

"You idiot," Randy yelled. "Kate nearly died because you told her there weren't peanuts in the dish."

Kate took in a giant gulp of air, feeling it burn her itchy throat. Sweet oxygen. Black spots continued to dance across her vision.

"I . . . I didn't think there was," Rosa said, her voice trembling. "My manager confirmed it was nut free. I even made a note for the chef."

"And what do you think now?" Randy demanded. "Where is your manager? I want to have a word with him."

A cool cloth dabbed her neck, and Kate looked up to see Taylor hovering over her with concerned eyes. He dipped the napkin into her water cup, then ran it along her arms.

"Are you with me?" he asked.

Slowly, Kate nodded, the movement taking all her effort. "It's helping," she wheezed.

It could've been three minutes or three hours before the front door of the restaurant burst open and two paramedics hustled inside, a gurney between them.

"Why do we always seem to find you in the middle of a crisis?" one of the paramedics asked Taylor. "What's happened here?"

"Anaphylaxis," Taylor said, rising. "I administered the epi-pen about five minutes ago. It seems to be helping, but not as much as it should."

Randy continued to scream at Rosa while Kate floated in and out of awareness. The manager was there now, his face white as Randy called them every name in the book. Kate wanted to curl into a ball underneath the table and hide from the hatred in his voice. Beau had yelled at her like that all too often.

"Can you tell me your name?" the paramedic asked as he shined a light in her eyes.

Kate blinked, forcing herself not to turn away. "Kaitlynn Monroe," she whispered.

"Good. We'll have you fixed up in no time."

Strong arms settled underneath her, and then Kate was lying on the gurney, being wheeled into the parking lot while Randy continued to yell at the manager and demand the waitress immediately be terminated from her position.

Kate felt a warm hand on her arm and looked up into Taylor's soft, worried eyes. "You'll be okay now," he said.

The ambulance doors opened, and Kate felt the gurney being lifted inside.

"Are you coming with us, Taylor?" the paramedic asked.

Taylor looked at Kate, his brow furrowed in concern.

"Don't leave me," she whispered.

He nodded and hopped into the back of the ambulance without another word. The lights flashed and the siren gave a stutter, and then they pulled out of the parking lot, leaving an irate Randy behind. Kate wondered how long it would take him to realize she was gone.

Chapter Nine

Taylor clutched Kate's hand as they raced through the congested streets of L.A. toward the hospital. The EMTs had placed an oxygen max over her face, but her color was still startlingly pale and her grip limp.

What if he hadn't been picking up takeout on his way home from the station? Kate's date would've stood there in a frozen panic while he watched her die.

The EMTs called out her vitals, but it did little to ease Taylor's concern. As a firefighter he had basic medical training, and logically he knew Kate would be okay. But there was still a part of him very worried for her safety.

Kate lifted the oxygen mask from her face. "I'm okay."

"We'll let the doctors tell us that," Taylor said. Her thin, weak voice did nothing to reassure him.

At the hospital, Kate was met by a doctor and wheeled inside. Taylor sat in a chair near her bed for two hours while they ran tests and labs. She seemed only half aware of what was happening.

The curtain pushed back, and a young doctor—probably still a resident—gave them a smile. "You're good to go, Mrs. Monroe," he said. "I've got your discharge papers right here. Just take it easy for the rest of the weekend. You should be fine to return to work on Monday." He glanced at Taylor, then back at Kate. "Do you have someone who can drive you home?"

"I'll take her," Taylor said. His truck was still back at the restaurant, but he'd hail a cab. Kate shouldn't be alone right now.

The doctor nodded. "I just need you to sign some paperwork, and then you can be on your way."

Twenty minutes later, Taylor helped Kate into the back of a cab.

"You really don't have to go with me," she protested. "I appreciate your help, but I'm fine now."

Taylor pinned her with a glare. "Please, give me more credit than that. I'd have to be some sort of monster to not make sure you get home okay after today."

He expected Kate to smile at the joke, but a frown puckered her forehead. Taylor shut her door, then walked around to the other side of the cab and got in.

"Where to?" the cabbie asked.

Taylor looked at Kate. "I know the general area, but I don't remember the exact address of your home."

Shadows flicked across her eyes, and she quickly rattled off the address. The cabbie nodded and pulled into the street.

"I'm not some damsel you need to save," Kate said. "I appreciate your help tonight, but I'm okay now. Don't feel like you have to help me out of some twisted sense of obligation."

Taylor's mouth dropped open. "Is that what you think this is to me—an obligation?"

She shrugged, not meeting his eyes. "You're a really nice guy, Taylor. But you're a firefighter. Rescuing people is in your blood. I'm not interested in being rescued—I'm interested in a real relationship. One that's based on more than a sense of chivalry."

"Oh, and is that what you were discovering tonight, with the date who couldn't even call 911?"

Kate's lips pursed together. "It was our first date. I think Randy was in shock."

"He didn't even notice when we left the restaurant. He was too busy screaming at the waitress who served you the dish."

"People handle stressful situations in different ways. I asked a stranger to come with me to the hospital, for example."

Taylor never would've guessed that quiet, timid Kate could be so stubborn.

"I think we've moved past stranger, and I'm not here purely out of a sense of chivalry," he said. "Or did you forget that I was the one who requested a second date?"

Kate's eyes widened, as though surprised he'd brought it up. "I didn't forget."

They turned down a quiet street and Taylor stopped talking, his eyes taking in the familiar road. Older-style homes ended in a cul-de-sac, with Kate's house at the very end.

The crackling sound of fire filled Taylor's ear, and he could hear Corey yelling, "Clear!" as they checked each room. Taylor had been the one to find Beau, unconscious in an armchair, and drag him outside. His heart had pounded frantically in his chest as sweat poured down his back from the blazing heat. His first fire. His first save. And ultimately, his first loss.

He hadn't had much time to observe the burning house, but he had noted the dry-rot on the front porch that had gone up instantly, the cheap plywood-style furniture that was reduced to nothing but ash. The layout of the house had screamed 1950s, and the kitchen appliances had suggested the house hadn't been updated since.

Now a quaint one-story house sat at the end of the driveway, looking warm and inviting with its gray stucco and stone. The xeriscaped front yard was modern and well-kept, and a colorful wreath of spring flowers hung on the door.

The cabbie pulled to a stop, and Taylor paid him despite Kate's protests. Then he took her by the arm and slowly led her up the walk to the front door.

"We should've had the cabbie take us to the restaurant so we could pick up our cars," Kate said, her voice tinged with exhaustion.

"I'll get Corey—the fireman with me at the safety fair—to help bring your car home tomorrow," Taylor said. "Tonight, you should just rest."

Her hands curled around the keys peaking out of her purse. "No, I can drive my own car."

"Okay," he said, not wanting to push her. "I can pick you up at least, then."

Kate unlocked the front door, and Taylor had his first glimpse into her new home. The entryway led into a living room, which gave way to the kitchen and dining area. Taylor instantly loved the open feel of the place and the gray laminate flooring throughout. The house that had burned had been so claustrophobic, with low ceilings and narrow hallways and rooms. This felt like a house Kate could breathe in. He was glad she'd been able to rebuild.

"I love your house," he said.

"Thanks." Kate dropped her purse onto the kitchen table, her face pale.

"Why don't you sit down? I'll get you something to eat."

Strike a Match

"I'm not hungry, thanks." Kate did as he suggested and sank into a couch overflowing with throw pillows. "I don't know if I ever want to eat again after tonight. I thought I was choosing a safe dish."

Taylor dropped onto the couch beside her. "You really had me worried."

"I bet the food somehow touched a surface that had peanuts on it. Maybe a new chef wasn't as careful as he should've been. I'm just glad it turned out okay in the end."

"Me too." Taylor gently brushed away a lock of her hair, then pulled back, realizing what he'd done.

"Thank you," Kate said quietly.

"I'm not here only because I feel a responsibility toward you. I know our past connection has got to be incredibly difficult to wrap your mind around. And I completely understand and respect that decision. But I asked to go out on another date with *you*, Kate. Not the widow of someone I couldn't save."

Kate's breath caught, and tears rimmed her eyes. "I like you too, Taylor. Maybe too much."

Hope sprang forth in his heart and he leaned forward, their faces mere inches apart. "Then what's the problem?"

She looked down. "You remind me of that night, but not in the way you think."

His brow furrowed in confusion. How many ways were there to remember that night? "Okay . . ."

"Beau was . . . not a nice man. Our relationship was rocky. When you told me he was gone, I felt . . ." She held her hands out, as though she could grasp the words from thin air. "I felt free."

"Did he hit you?" Taylor asked, trying to keep his voice soft instead of angry.

She blinked, and a single tear slid down her cheek. "No, nothing like that. But his words hurt as much as any punch. I feel guilty every day for not missing Beau more." She dropped her gaze, her voice almost a whisper. "I feel guilty for being so attracted to you."

Kate had been abused. Not physically, perhaps, but emotionally. Suddenly everything clicked into place, so much of her previous behavior making perfect sense. Anger roared inside Taylor, as strong as any fire, along with a fierce need to protect Kate. To make all her pain disappear.

He was glad Beau was gone.

Taylor reached out, catching a tear on the tip of his fingertip. "I want to take you on another date. Will you let me?"

Kate closed her eyes, her shoulders rising as she breathed deeply. "I don't know if that's a good idea."

"I think it's the best idea. Please, Kate. Let me take you on a date, something to make up for that first awful one. Let me show you how normal we can be."

Her eyes opened, their emerald green depths holding more emotion than he could even attempt to read. She searched his face while Taylor held his breath. She was going to refuse. He couldn't blame her, really. No doubt she wanted to forget anything and anyone connected to her past.

After what felt like an eternity, she gave one, quick nod. "Okay."

Hope soared in Taylor's heart, and he grinned. He'd meant to go on the date and forget about Kate forever. But she was anything but forgettable. Her quiet strength was more attractive than he'd ever dreamed it could be.

He wanted to lean forward and brush his lips against hers so badly he ached, but instead he stood. Now was not the time. If he wanted a chance with Kate—a real chance at something permanent—then he needed to take it slow. "I should let you rest. Can I help you with anything before I leave?"

"No, I'll be fine."

"Can I get your number at least?"

She gave a small nod, and it felt like a major victory. Taylor quickly entered her number in. "Call me when you wake up in the morning, and we can go get your car."

Kate stood and walked him to the door. Her pace was slow but steady, making him feel a little better about leaving her alone. "How will you get home?"

Lindzee Armstrong

"I texted Corey while we were in the cab. He should be here to pick me up any minute. We'll stop by the restaurant and grab my car."

"You don't have to wait outside."

Taylor tenderly took Kate's face in his hands, staring into her eyes. He leaned forward and let his lips gently brush her cheek. "Yes, I do. Goodnight, Kate. I'll see you tomorrow."

He drove to the restaurant on clouds, ignoring all of Corey's ribbing. Once in his condo, Taylor fed Ember, then sat down at his computer to check his email. He deleted three coupons and ignored an email from Brooke with another profile. He wasn't interested in dating anyone else.

He scrolled down to the next batch of emails and froze. An email from the San Diego Fire Department. Slowly he opened the email. They wanted to interview him in person next week.

Taylor sat back in the chair and ran a hand through his hair. Even a week ago, he would've taken the interview without a thought. But Kate had somehow changed everything.

He picked up his phone, going through the last few texts from Amy. Requests for money, drunken texts that made no sense, pleas for help with various things. She needed a bus pass. She'd been fired from her job after only two days—the job he'd dedicated an entire weekend to helping her get. The A/C in her unit was broken, but the landlord wouldn't repair it until her rent was current.

He closed his eyes, holding the phone to his chest. He'd done everything he could to help her, but she continued to spiral. Did that mean his parents were right and he needed to back off?

No. If he lived in San Diego, he could convince Amy to stop drinking. If she moved in with him, he'd be able to keep an eye on her. Make sure she stayed sober and didn't fall back into her old habits.

He'd known Kate a week. He'd known Amy his entire life. She was more than his sister—she was his twin. And he wouldn't abandon her for a girl he'd been out with only once.

An interview didn't mean they'd offer him the job. But he had to give it his best shot.

He clicked reply.

Chapter Ten

When Kate woke up the next morning, it was to a painfully scratchy throat and itchy skin. But at least she could breathe again. Last night had been . . . scary. Humiliating. Embarrassing.

Comforting.

What would she have done if Taylor hadn't been there to administer the epi-pen and call an ambulance? Randy had totally frozen when faced with conflict, which didn't bother Kate near as much as how he'd treated the waitress, who'd done nothing wrong. Randy's behavior, as Kate was being carted out to the ambulance on a gurney, had reminded her too much of Beau. And she didn't want any part of a relationship that reminded her—even a little—of her late husband.

Taking a shower exhausted her, so Kate contented herself with pulling her hair up in a simple bun and swiping on a dab of lip gloss. She'd only recently started wearing makeup again, or even doing much with her hair for that matter. But somehow, the possibility of seeing Taylor today had her wishing she had the energy to make herself look a little more put together. But maybe it was better this way. She didn't want to look like she was trying too hard and give him the wrong idea. Although she had agreed to go out with him again, so the point was probably moot.

By ten o'clock, Kate was wondering if she'd misunderstood Taylor. They hadn't exactly agreed on a time for him to come and get her. She supposed she could call, but that felt too forward. She was just about to call Liza, or maybe a cab company so she wouldn't have to answer awkward questions, when her phone buzzed with a text.

Taylor: I hope I'm not waking you up.
Kate: No, I've been up for a while.
Taylor: How are you feeling?

Kate smiled, clutching the phone tight. *Fine,* she quickly texted back. *Tired, but no lasting effects. I'll be all better by Monday.*

Taylor: Is it okay if I come pick you up in about fifteen minutes, then? We can go get your car.

Kate texted back a quick reply, then put on a little eyeshadow and mascara.

The knock at the door immediately sent butterflies swarming her stomach. Taylor looked relaxed and comfortable in jeans and a blue tee.

"Morning," Taylor said.

"Morning." Kate locked her front door, then followed Taylor to his truck.

"You look like you're feeling better," Taylor said, holding open the passenger side door. "Your coloring isn't as pale. I know I wouldn't look half as good the morning after being so ill."

"I'm fine, really. I haven't had a reaction in at least two years." She'd been hyper vigilant, knowing she was all alone. Beau hadn't been able to move quickly enough to help her during an attack anyway. Besides, if she was ill, who would take care of Beau? She'd had two attacks during their time together—one when they were engaged, and one a few years into their marriage. Caring for a convalescent was challenging enough without being one herself.

"You really scared me," Taylor said. "I've never seen someone go into anaphylactic shock before."

"Thank you again for helping me."

"I wish I could take you out to lunch or something afterward, but I agreed to take over a shift for a guy at the station so he could go to his grandma's birthday party."

"You don't owe me lunch," Kate said. "It's nice of you to help out a coworker."

"I don't mind. I love my job at the station. Besides, it's not like we're fighting fires all day. Most of the time we're just sitting around or running drills."

The twenty-minute drive flew by as they chatted, and soon they were at the restaurant.

"Thanks for driving me," Kate said.

"Of course." Taylor reached over, gently grasping her hand so she couldn't open the passenger-side door. "I meant what I said last night. I'd really like to take you out again, Kate."

"I'll talk to Brooke," Kate said quietly.

Taylor nodded and released her, a grin on his face. "I'll follow you to make sure you get home safely."

"That's really not necessary. I can just send you a text when I get there."

"I insist. You're looking a little pale again, and I'm not taking any chances."

"Okay." Kate wasn't used to someone being concerned about her welfare. But today she'd try being grateful instead of snippy. "Thank you."

Taylor's truck stayed visible in her rearview mirror the entire drive home. Kate's stomach fluttered with happy nerves. It felt good to have someone worried about whether or not she got home safely, instead of yelling at her for showing up late.

Kate pulled into her garage and got out of the driveway, expecting to see Taylor gone. But he idled on her curb, the window down.

"Are you sure you'll be okay by yourself?" he asked.

Kate nodded. She did feel a little dizzy and lightheaded, but she knew it would pass if she spent a few hours resting. "Thank you again."

"Of course. I'll be seeing you soon." He gave her a heart-stopping grin, then waved as he drove away.

She was in serious trouble. Her heart was behaving in a way it hadn't in years.

Kate laid down on the living room couch and turned the television to the home improvement channel, letting herself drift. The ringing of her phone jerked her out of a pleasant fantasy in which she and Taylor were watching the sunrise from a mountain peak. Kate fumbled for her phone and answered it with a groggy, "Hello?"

"Oh my gosh, Kate. I just got into the office and listened to the voice mail from Randy. Are you okay? What happened?"

Kate rubbed her eyes, struggling to place the voice. "I'm sorry, who is this?"

"Brooke. From Toujour."

Toujour! Kate sat up, suddenly more alert. "Sorry, it's been a long few hours. I'm still not thinking clearly."

"Do you have a few minutes we can talk?" Brooke said. "I didn't mean to pounce on you like that. I was just so worried. Did I wake you up?"

"It's fine." Kate picked up the remote and muted the television. "I've been resting, not sleeping. I'm not doing anything right now. We can talk."

"Randy feels awful," Brooke said. "He said he was talking to the manager and waitress about what had happened, and when he turned around, you were gone. Of course he wanted to call and apologize himself, but he doesn't have your number."

Kate nodded, not surprised. At Toujour, client information was kept strictly private, and it was up to each person to decide what contact information they did or did not share with their date.

"Can I ask what happened?" Brooke continued. "I have Randy's side of the story, but I'd like yours."

So Kate related the incident, including her assumption that the chicken had been fried in peanut oil, which had caused her allergic reaction.

"And how did you feel Randy handled the situation?" Brooke asked.

Kate chewed on her lip. "He was obviously very concerned."

"Kate, I can't help you on your journey to love if you won't be honest with me. We can learn a lot about a person in a crisis. What did you learn about Randy?"

Kate sighed, deciding to be honest. "He froze up at first, but that's not what disturbed me. He was being very aggressive toward the waitress and manager. I was only half-coherent, but I still heard him yelling that she should be fired. Everything was kind of foggy, but his tone of voice made me nervous." Too much like Beau.

"That's completely understandable." Brooke was quiet for a moment. "I spoke with Taylor this morning as well. He said he happened to be there and went with you to the hospital."

Kate blushed, pulling the blanket up to her flaming cheeks. "He was a perfect gentleman. I'm very grateful he was there."

"He still wants to go out with you, but what do you want?"

"I . . . I think I'm ready for a second date with Taylor. I'm not interested in pursuing a relationship with Randy."

Kate could almost hear Brooke's smile across the phone. "Excellent. We can talk more about this at your scheduled appointment on Monday. But I'll talk to Taylor and get something set up right away."

Chapter Eleven

Kate couldn't believe how the last month had flow by. She and Taylor had been out on three dates, but she'd also been out on a first date with two other guys. Taylor was by far the most interesting of the men—and also the only one who made her heart flutter.

But the ghost of Beau still haunted her. Despite the fact that she and Taylor were having a great time together, and their relationship seemed to be progressing, Kate was terrified to commit. She'd thought she and Beau were a perfect match, and look where that ended up. But at some point, she would have to take that leap of faith.

She wanted to leap with Taylor.

He glanced over at her and smiled, sending a *zing* through her entire body. An arm rested casually out his truck window as he drove toward his childhood home in a suburb of L.A.

Yeah. She was meeting his parents—and maybe his sister, too. Taylor was excited because he'd bought Amy a bus ticket and thought she might show up. Kate hadn't initially considered what meeting his family meant when she agreed to go to the Memorial Day barbecue with him. She'd been too worried about the fact that Memorial Day happened to be Beau's birthday. But now she was excited for more in-depth glimpse into Taylor's life. She had a feeling he'd ask her to put her profile on hold this weekend.

"You okay?" Taylor asked.

Kate forced a smile. "Yes, just thinking."

"Only good thoughts, I hope."

"Of course." Kate shifted in her seat, anxiety growing as they turned off the main road and down a quiet residential street. They had to be getting close.

"My parents are really nice. They won't harass you too much, promise. And you'll love Amy. The rest of the people will just be friends and neighbors."

Kate nodded, trying not to let anxiety crowd out the joy of being with Taylor. She'd never really had to meet family when it came to Beau. He'd ran away from home when he was a teenager and lost contact with his parents and siblings. She'd tried to get him to contact his family time and time again, but it hadn't been until after his death she'd finally tracked them down.

Today Beau would've been thirty-three. Kate hadn't realized that until a split second after agreeing to this date. Guilt had instantly consumed her for not remembering, and Taylor had promised he wouldn't be offended if she backed out. But she'd started this journey to move past Beau, and saying "no" to Taylor because of an arbitrary calendar date felt like a step backward. She'd woken up that morning feeling nostalgic for the good days with Beau—and there had been good days, especially during their brief engagement—but the excitement of seeing Taylor had quickly overtaken her.

"Here we are." Taylor pulled up in front of a quaint two-story home and killed the engine. "Home sweet home."

Kate slowly got out of the truck, looking up at the house. It was obviously older, with peeling paint around the door frame and a brick exterior that had long ago gone out of vogue. But the home also looked loved and cared for. Flowers flourishes in the garden bed underneath the wide front window, and the mailbox had the name *Coleman* hand-stenciled on it with butterflies fluttering around the name.

Taylor stuck his hands in his pockets, shoulders hunched. "It's not much."

"I think it's wonderful," Kate said. Her grandparents had tried their hardest, but they'd been way past the prime of their life. Consequently, most of the housework and home repair projects were done by Kate or not done at all.

"Well, shall we?" Taylor held out a hand, and Kate slowly placed hers inside his strong grasp. They'd held hands a few times now, but each encounter made her feel simultaneously exultant and guilty.

"Are you sure you're okay?" Taylor asked. "I know this is a hard day for you."

"I'm fine." Kate plastered on a big smile. "Let's go meet your parents." Maybe her future in-laws. She gulped at the thought. She and Taylor were nowhere close to discussing marriage, but they were both clients of Toujour and marriage was the obvious end game.

Taylor opened the front door without knocking. The house was empty and quiet, but muffled laughter drifted in from the backyard. Kate barely had time to take in the shag carpet and faded floral-print furniture in the living room before Taylor led her down a narrow hallway. She caught a glimpse of a small kitchen with faded white cabinets and dated wallpaper before he opened the back door and ushered her outside.

Unlike the house, the backyard was expansive, an inviting oasis with mature shade trees and a fire pit area that looked brand new. Adults milled around the yard, some holding babies and others canes, as young children ran around playing some sort of game. A gentle murmur filled the space, and Kate wanted to cry.

This felt like coming home.

Taylor gave her hand a small squeeze, and Kate clung to that hand, worried that if she let go this would all disappear. This is what a functional family with roots and friends looked like. Kate wanted this life for herself more than anything.

She needed Taylor.

Ice leeched away the joy that had filled her heart moments before as panic took its place. The idea of needing anyone was terrifying.

She shouldn't have come. Especially not on Beau's birthday.

"Come meet my parents," Taylor said, pulling her toward a middle-aged couple with round figures and smiling faces.

Kate shyly pulled to a stop beside Taylor, suddenly wishing she'd worn more makeup or maybe bought a new outfit for today. She wanted to make a good impression so badly.

"Mom, Dad," Taylor said. "This is Kate. Kate meet my parents, Harold and Ada."

"It's so nice to meet you," Ada said, the smile on her face genuine. "We've heard so much about you."

"Only good things," Harold added. "We're glad you're here. Burgers will be ready any minute now."

"I guess you haven't heard from Amy, have you?" Ada asked, directing her attention back to Taylor. "She said she'd be here."

"She'll call me when she gets to the bus station and I'll go pick her up."

Ada frowned. "Are you sure she's com—"

"Oh, look, there's Tom," Taylor said. He smiled at Kate. "He's been our next door neighbor my entire life. I'd better go introduce you." Taylor dragged her away before his parents could protest. "Sorry," he said. "But every time they bring up Amy, we just end up arguing. I hope it's not a disaster having her here."

"I'm sorry," Kate said. She knew all too well what it was like to have an addict as a family member.

"I wish they would help her more."

She squeezed his hand. "Have you heard anything more from San Diego?"

"Uh, yeah." He cleared his throat. "I wasn't planning on bringing it up here, but they offered me the job."

She pulled him to a stop, her eyes widening. "Are you going to take it?"

He tugged her forward. "We don't need to talk about it now. I know this isn't an easy day for you, and I don't want to add to the stress. Let's just enjoy the party, okay? I'm really excited to introduce you to some of these people."

Kate nodded. San Diego wasn't so far away—maybe he wanted to give long distance a try. He wouldn't bring her to meet his parents if he planned on never seeing her again. She pushed aside her worry and followed Taylor around the yard, smiling as he introduced her to friends whose names she forgot almost instantly.

They'd been there almost an hour when Taylor's phone started ringing. He picked it up, his expression falling. "It's Amy. I've got to take this."

"No problem." Kate didn't like the way his eyes had filled with anxiety at his sister's name.

Taylor answered the phone, his voice edged with worry. "Hello? Yeah, I'm here. Where are you? Mom's been asking me when you'll get here . . . Wait, are you drunk? I'm not mad, I just want to know. Where are you? . . . So you never got on the bus? Yeah . . . Yeah . . . Call your friend and see if she can help. Then call me back, okay?" Taylor clicked the phone off, shoving it back in his pocket.

"Something wrong?" Kate asked, already knowing the answer.

"Amy didn't get on the bus. She's wasted at some bar in San Diego. She isn't even sure which one, but the bartender is kicking her out and she doesn't have money for cab fare. And she got evicted from her apartment this morning. I'm so mad at the landlord. He told me he wouldn't when I wrote him the check, as long as she kept paying." He gave a humorless laugh. "I guess I have my answer to that riddle. Her rent was due this week."

"I'm sorry," Kate said.

Strike a Match

"I do everything I can to help her, but she's only getting worse."

"Did you say Amy called?" a deep voice asked.

Taylor let out a quiet curse and turned toward his dad. "Yeah, that was her. I don't think she'll make it to the party after all."

Harold let out a sigh. "Where is she?"

Taylor folded his arms, and his defensive stance had Kate's heart pounding in her chest. "What does it matter? You aren't going to help her."

"She's still my daughter, and I love her."

"Then help her, Dad."

"No one can help Amy until she's willing to help herself. Haven't you figured that out yet?"

Taylor's phone started buzzing again, and he flicked it on with a growl. When he hung up a moment later, he said, "Sorry, that was work. Someone's sick, and I need to cover their shift. We have to go."

It wasn't the first time Taylor had cut their time together short to help someone else out. Kate had been understanding the other times. But today? She took a shaky breath, watching Harold's face grow red with anger.

"Oh, and I'm sure there was no one else at the station who could cover for you," Harold said. "Instead of respecting your date" —he nodded his head toward Kate, and she wanted to shrivel up like a weed and blow away in the wind— "you're abandoning us to help someone who can help themselves. Again."

Kate's heart pounded in a chest tight with anxiety. She didn't like the conflict of this moment—didn't like the side of Taylor that was emerging. Was he really going to rush off to help someone else, knowing how hard a day this was for Kate? And what about Amy?

"Goodbye, Dad." Taylor grabbed Kate's hand and pulled her toward the house.

They didn't talk as Taylor helped her into the truck. As he headed toward the freeway, Kate's mind whirled. She understood why Taylor wanted to help his sister. But Kate knew first-hand that helping an alcoholic only ended in disaster. She shivered, suddenly cold despite the May heat.

"Is someone really sick at work?" Kate asked.

Taylor shrugged. "Probably not. This guy fakes illness a lot so he and his girlfriend can spend the weekend in Vegas. But I hate saying no just in case. And I had to get away from my dad."

Kate curled her fingers toward her palms, feeling nauseated. He was cutting their date short so some guy could get drunk and blow money at slot machines in Vegas? Leaving the party to help his sister she understood, even if she didn't agree. But this?

Taylor pulled up to her house and cut the engine, getting out. He silently walked her up the path to her front door, and Kate fumbled with her keys, then unlocked it.

"Sorry I had to cut our date short," Taylor said. "Let's plan something for tomorrow night, okay? I should be home by dawn, unless I need to go to San Diego and help Amy. We can talk about the job then."

"Okay," Kate said. She turned the doorknob and stepped inside, then paused. "No, you know what? I don't have to take this from you. It's not okay, Taylor. I can't believe you're leaving me on today—my late husband's birthday—to take the shift of some frat boy who never grew up. I can't believe, after all the guilt I've experienced this past week for agreeing to the date, this is how it ends. But more than that, I can't believe that you're willing to help some casual acquaintance, but not your own sister. Because you may think you're helping her, but you're dad's right—you're enabling her. It's easier for you to play the kind big brother than to do the hard thing and tell her no. You're taking the easy way out, and that's not the type of guy I want a relationship with. Not again."

Taylor's mouth fell open, shock lining his features. "Kate, I—"

"Goodbye, Taylor," Kate said. And then she shut the door.

Chapter Twelve

Taylor tore down the freeway, aggressively cutting off drivers and weaving through traffic as he headed toward the station. His parents made him so angry. No, they infuriated him. Amy infuriated him. He missed his twin sister—the girl who had teased him about playing dolls and had given him hugs when he fell off his bike and scraped his knee. He'd do anything to get that girl back.

He'd thought he'd finally met someone who would understand when he started dating Kate. Her family was even more dysfunctional than his. With a drug-addicted dad in prison and a mother that was probably dead of an overdose, surely she'd understand why he had to do everything possible to help Amy the way his parents wouldn't.

Except Amy was still getting worse. He'd spent a decade doing it his way with no results. Was Kate right? Were his parents?

Taylor pulled to a stop in the parking lot of the fire station, then grabbed his bag from the back of the truck and stalked inside. Maybe he had been wrong to leave Kate, especially on such a difficult day. But it wasn't like he'd abandoned her at the party and left her to find her own way home. He'd explained the situation, then driven her back to her place and walked her to the door like a gentleman. If she couldn't handle the unpredictable life of someone in service to the public, then maybe it was better if they ended things now.

Except he didn't want to end things and move to San Diego. He wanted to stay right here in L.A. with her.

Taylor walked through the front doors of the fire station, surprised to see Corey sitting at the kitchen table.

"What are you doing here?" Taylor asked.

Corey folded his arms and leaned back in his chair. "My shift isn't over for another ten minutes. What are you doing here?"

"Doug claims he's sick again and asked me to take his shift."

Corey pursed his lips. "I thought you were taking Kate to your parents' house."

"Yeah, we did go there for a while." Taylor tossed his bag to the ground and sank into a chair next to Corey. "I don't know, man. Things were going great, and then Amy had to call and ruin everything. I got in a fight with my dad, and then Kate blew up at me when I dropped her off."

"Can't say I blame her. Cutting the date short was a pretty jerk move."

"Doug's sick. What am I supposed to do?"

Corey snorted. "You and I both know Doug isn't sick of anything but working. Didn't you say today was kind of a rough day for Kate? She should be angry. You left her—the girl you're dating—when she really needed you to help someone with a complete disregard for responsibility. Why is it that you'll help complete strangers, but you won't help those you love?"

Love. The word echoed through Taylor's mind, and a lump formed in his throat. Did he really love Kate? They'd been dating such a short amount of time, but he definitely felt something strong for her.

"It's not that black and white," Taylor said.

"It is, man. What makes today so important to Kate?"

Taylor looked down, the guilt welling inside him. "It's her husband's birthday."

Corey stared at Taylor, then swore. "You're a piece of work. It'll serve you right if she dumps your sorry butt."

"We're barely even dating." But Taylor had no desire to see what other women Toujour had to offer him. He already knew he'd found the one he wanted.

"If I were Kate, I wouldn't want to date you either. She needs someone who's going to be there for her, no matter what. Not someone with a misguided hero complex who's always rushing off to someone else's aid."

Taylor sighed. "It's not just that. She said I enable Amy. That she doesn't want to be with a guy who does that."

"Kate's a smart woman."

"Excuse me?"

"Amy's an alcoholic. She needs to be checked into a treatment program. Instead you give her money every time she drinks all hers away."

"If I can just—"

"You can't help someone who doesn't help themselves. I don't blame Kate for not wanting to be with someone who only gives to the wrong people. Moving to San Diego would be the worst possible thing you could do for Amy. She'll have no reason to stay sober if you're there babysitting her."

Taylor stared at Corey as clarity sharpened his vision of Amy—and of Kate. Two futures played out before him, making his stomach churn. If he moved to San Diego, Amy would continue to get worse. His life would revolve around dragging her home from bars and hoping she didn't end up dead from her addiction.

But if he stayed here in Los Angeles, he could finally break the cycle. Maybe, if he followed his parents' lead, Amy would finally get the help she needed. And maybe Taylor would get Kate, if he hadn't screwed things up too badly.

Fear swept through Taylor and he rose. "You have to take Doug's shift for me."

"What? I've already been here for two days."

"Just a few hours. Please, Corey. I have to talk to Kate."

Corey sighed, but Taylor saw the small smile he was trying to hide. "Fine. Go try and fix things with your girl. But then come right back here. I've got plans with Amanda tonight, and I'm not dumb enough to cancel them for Doug."

"Thank you." Taylor raced out of the station and hopped in his truck. He had to get to Kate.

He made it to her house in record time, stopping only once at the grocery store a block away from her house for flowers. He raced up the steps to her front porch and rapped sharply on the door. His breathing was loud in his ears, but silence echoed from the house.

His shoulders slumped. Had she left to run errands? Then a worse thought hit him. Maybe she was inside the house and choosing not to open the door.

He rapped on the door again. She wouldn't brush him off that easily. "Please, Kate. I'm sorry. I made a mistake. Let me in so I can apologize."

The door flew open, and Taylor took a quick step back. Kate stood in the doorway, her arms folded across her stomach and green eyes blazing. They stared at each other for a moment, electricity sizzling between them.

"Well?" Kate said. "I thought you wanted to apologize. Start talking."

Taylor swallowed, thrusting the flowers toward her. She took them slowly, no hint of relenting in her expression.

"I'm sorry," Taylor said. "I was a complete and total jerk. My parents have been saying the same thing as you for years, and lately I've started wondering if they're right. But it didn't click until I heard it from you. I should try harder to help my sister—*really* help her—even though I know it'll be hard not to rush to her side every time she asks for help. I should put the needs of those I love over the needs of those I barely know."

"You can't save the entire world, Taylor. I need someone who will pick his battles. And I need to be one of those battles every time."

He swallowed hard. "I know. I'm so sorry I left. I'm sorry I wasn't more sensitive to how hard of a day this was for you. I can't promise that I won't continue to make mistakes. But I can promise that I'll try my hardest every day to put your needs above anyone else's. Because that's what a relationship is about. And that's what I want from you—a real relationship. The whole package. I want to put your needs first."

Kate clutched the flowers to her chest. "What are you saying?"

He took a bold step forward, crossing the threshold of her home. "I'm saying I love you, Kate. I love watching you stand up for yourself, even when it's hard. I love your quiet strength. I love the way you take care of others, the way you love your job. I love the way you're willing to be honest with me, even when it's not what I want to hear. I don't want you to date anyone else. Just the thought makes me sick inside. I'm ready to put my profile on hold at Toujour and pursue this relationship wholeheartedly. I'm ready to deal with the difficult parts and work through the challenges that may arise. I'm all in."

Tears trickled down Kate's cheeks and she blinked, quickly wiping them away. "I'm scared to trust you. Because I know if I let myself, I'll fall—hard. And I don't know if my heart can handle being broken again."

"I could never break your heart." Taylor slowly reached out, taking the flowers from her hands and setting them on the coffee table.

"That's what they all say."

"You have to let me in, Kate. Take that leap and trust me. I promise, I'm not going to let you fall." He took her hands and slowly drew her toward him.

Kate collapsed against him, shoulders shaking. Relief coursed through Taylor and he mouthed a silent *thank you* to the heavens as he held her close. He rubbed slow circles on her back, whispering soothing words.

"I think I love you, too," Kate said. "And it terrifies me."

Taylor took her face gently between his hands. "Does that mean you'll put your profile on hold?"

Kate closed her eyes. "Does this mean you aren't taking the job in San Diego?"

Taylor swallowed hard. He would still help Amy. But this time, he would give her the right kind of help. And he wouldn't upend his life for her. He wouldn't abandon Kate for Amy. "I'm not going anywhere."

Kate's green eyes glistened, and she gave a small smile. "Okay then."

"Okay?"

"I'll put my profile on hold."

Taylor raised his eyes to the ceiling, a laugh filling him. When he looked back at Kate, she was smiling too.

"I guess this means we're officially a couple," Taylor said.

"Yeah, I guess it does."

"I love you, Kate."

"I think I love you, too."

Taylor slowly lowered his lips towards hers, heart soaring. He paused, giving her a chance to pull away.

She didn't.

His lips pressed against hers and he instantly knew that there was no turning back. He was hers forever.

Her lips were soft as a feather, and he could taste the salt of tears on them. He hated that he'd caused them, and vowed to do better from here on out. He would be the man that she deserved.

Kate wrapped her arms around his neck, her body soft and warm against his, lips exerting just the right amount of pressure. Her auburn locks were like silk sliding through his fingers. Taylor was desperate to stay in this moment forever, but he knew she needed to take things slow. He gave her one last, long kiss then pulled back.

Kate placed a hand on the back of his neck, pulling him in once more. And he knew that he'd just found the rest of his life.

Epilogue

Five Months Later

Kate let out a ragged breath, her calves burning with the intensity of the incline.

Taylor looked back at her, grinning. "Almost there," he said. "The view is worth the hike. I promise."

"It better be," Kate said, but she kept her tone teasing. This hike was the toughest they'd conquered yet, a two-hour climb that at times was almost vertical. Her lungs burned from exertion, and her body was covered in a thin sheen of sweat, despite the cooler October temperatures. She'd pulled off her jacket and wrapped it around her waist over an hour ago.

"Hurry," Taylor said. "We can't miss the sunrise after all this. Just one more hill."

She took his outstretched hand, loving the feel of his strong fingers holding hers. "I'm not about to miss it," she said. Then, digging deep, she found her last reserves of strength and pushed through the pain, cresting the final hill a step ahead of Taylor. She inhaled sharply, then let out a small, "Oh." The entire city of Los Angeles sprawled below them. The sun was just beginning to peek over the ocean, bathing the water in glittering light.

She put a hand to her heart, fighting tears. She felt a little like that ocean, finally glowing with light after what felt like an eternity in darkness. Taylor had helped her find that sunlight. And while he was a big part of why she was so content, she knew that she'd always had the power to make her own happiness. She'd just needed to learn how.

"Taylor, it's beautiful," Kate said, reaching behind her for his hand but not finding it. "Totally worth the hike. Taylor?" She turned around, not wanting him to miss this.

Taylor knelt before her in the hard dirt, dark hair wild from the hike and a smudge of dirt across one muscled shoulder. And in his hands he held a ring box. He smiled, the cleft in his chin becoming more pronounced as his eyes sparkled.

Kate's heart pounded in her chest, but for once it was a good thing. Tears pricked at her eyes and a hand flew to her mouth.

"Kate Monroe, I love you," Taylor said. "Our relationship's been a little like this hike—sometimes rocky, sometimes hard, but intensely beautiful and more than worth the climb. I want nothing more than to spend the rest of my life conquering challenges with you by my side. Will you marry me?"

"Yes!" Kate flung herself at Taylor. He caught her with a laugh, pulling her to the dirt beside him. He pulled the ring out of the box, a brilliant single solitaire diamond on a gold band, and slipped it onto her finger.

"I love you," Taylor said, brushing a sweaty strand of hair behind her ear.

"I love you, too," Kate said. "You've been so good to me over the last six months. I know I come with a lot of baggage. But you've never complained at the pace I've set. I've fallen more in love with you as I've watched you practice tough love on your sister. As I've watched you set boundaries at work, even though it's hard. As I've watched you help those who can't help themselves." She placed a hand on his cheek. "I don't know what I did to deserve you."

"We were made for each other, Kate. And I can't wait to spend the rest of our lives showing you just how perfect we are together."

She knew she looked awful. Her hair and clothes were damp with sweat, her face was probably streaked with dirt, and she was dressed in a baggy shirt and loose jeans with holes in the knees. But she knew Taylor saw through her bruised, battered self to who she really was. And he loved her not in spite of her struggles, but because of them.

Kate leaned into Taylor, and he wrapped his arms tightly around her. As they watched the sun rise over the valley, she knew this was the beginning of a new—and beautiful—chapter of her life. One she appreciated all the more because of her struggles.

She couldn't wait to get started.

FREE DOWNLOAD

Nothing slows down love like the friend zone.

amazonkindle ☆☆☆☆☆ ▾   4.4 out of 5 stars

"This was the book I've been looking for!"
—Angela, reader

Get your free copy of *Meet Your Match* when you opt in to the author's VIP reader's club. **Get started here:**

http://lindzeearmstrong.com/claim-your-free-book

Enjoy the Rest of the Series!

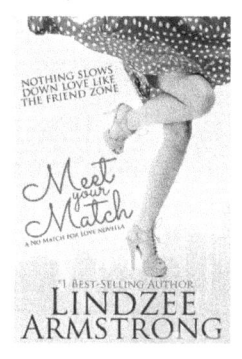

Sometimes love needs a helping hand...

www.LindzeeArmstrong.com

Meet Your Match: *Nothing slows love down like the friend zone.* Brooke's convinced all boys are trouble. Luke's a player who loves the thrill of the chase. Can a set of crazy rules keep these two safely in the friend zone? *Enjoy this witty and fast-paced romance today!*

Miss Match: *Playing cupid may break her heart.* With the matchmaking company she works for in decline, Brooke is desperate to sign Luke, her billionaire best friend, as a client. But Luke is more interested in capturing Brooke's heart. *Escape into this lighthearted romantic comedy today, which InD'Tale Magazine calls a "feel-good romance that will leave you swooning."*

Not Your Match: *Sometimes it takes dating Mr. Wrong to find Mr. Right.* Dating the wrong people has convinced both Ben and Andi that what they really want is each other. All that's standing in their way is a fake boyfriend, a jealous ex-fiancée, and being afraid to risk their hearts. *Explore this emotionally-charged romance today!*

Mix 'N Match: *Fire and ice aren't meant to mix.* Zoey and Mitch couldn't be more opposite. One passionate kiss has convinced them they'd never work. But three weeks in Paris could change everything. *Take a trip to Paris in this fun-filled romantic comedy today!*

Mistletoe Match: *A kiss shouldn't be this complicated.* When animal rights activist Michelle kisses a mystery man underneath the mistletoe at a holiday party, she's horrified to realize he's the new marketing director of the pharmaceutical company she's trying to destroy due to their nasty habit of animal testing. Can one impulsive kiss be the foundation for a happily ever after? *Curl up with this delicious holiday romance today!*

OTHER BOOKS BY LINDZEE ARMSTRONG

Sunset Plains Romance Series

Cupcakes and Cowboys

Twisters and Textbooks

Other Works

First Love, Second Choice

Chasing Someday

Cupcakes and Cowboys: *He's everything that broke her heart.* Cassidy wants two things—to make her cupcake shop a success, and to forget that her fiancé traded her for the lights of Hollywood. When Jase—best friend of her ex and A-list actor—shows up at the ranch to research an upcoming role, forgetting is the last thing she can do. Can Jase convince her he's really a country boy at heart? *Devour this deliciously romantic story today!*

Twisters and Textbooks: *Some storms can't be outrun.* After the death of her parents, chasing tornadoes is the only thing that makes Lauren feel alive. Each storm gives her the adrenaline rush she craves, but it can't make her forget Tanner, the country boy she left behind in Oklahoma. When a tornado brings the couple back together, Lauren and Tanner are caught up in a cyclone of emotions neither is sure they want to escape. Can they weather the storm of their past, or will they let it consume them? *Get caught up in this wildly romantic story today!*

First Love, Second Choice: What happens when you impersonate your identical twin sister to score a date with your long-lost high school crush? *Enjoy this delightfully sweet case of mistaken identity today!*

Chasing Someday: Infertility stinks. No one knows that better than Megan, Christina, and Kyra. As these three women become accidental friends, they realize that what you see isn't necessarily what's beneath the surface. And some secrets aren't worth the cost of keeping them. *Immerse yourself in this emotionally charged story today!*

About the Author

LINDZEE ARMSTRONG is the #1 best-selling author of the No Match for Love series and Sunset Plains Romance series. She's always had a soft spot for love stories. In third grade, she started secretly reading romance novels, hiding the covers so no one would know (because hello, embarrassing!), and dreaming of her own Prince Charming.

She finally met her true love while at college, where she studied history education. They are now happily married and raising twin boys in the Rocky Mountains.

Like any true romantic, Lindzee loves chick flicks, ice cream, and chocolate. She believes in sigh-worthy kisses and happily ever afters, and loves expressing that through her writing.

To find out about future releases, you can join Lindzee's VIP reader's club by visiting her website at www.lindzeearmstrong.com.

If you enjoyed this book, please take a few minutes and leave a review. This is the best way you can say thank you to an author! It really helps other readers discover books they might enjoy. Thank you!

Harris County Public Library
Houston, Texas